Advance praise for *Earning It* by Angela Quarles

"Sizzles with heat, sparkles with charm...you'll savor every sexy, emotion-packed moment!"
— Julie Anne Long, USA Today best selling author of the Hellcat Canyon series

"Fun and flirty, EARNING IT is a winner!"
— Avery Flynn, *USA Today* best selling author of *The Negotiator*

"Get ready to swoon hard for a Navy SEAL! Angela Quarles' first contemporary romance is hot and funny and delivers everything I want in a sexy read. This series is a feast of military and sports heroes—the best possible combination for romance readers!"
— Ainsley Booth, *USA Today* bestselling author of *Prime Minister*

"Sweet and steamy, Earning It is a super fun take on the mistaken identity theme set against an unusual sports romance backdrop. A great read!"
— Kate Meader, *USA Today* bestselling author of the Hot in Chicago series

"Pepper and Luke sizzle...my e-reader almost caught fire during a few sexy scenes. This read was sweetness and smolder with just the right dash of swoon. Whip-smart writing and sly humor abounds-simply my favorite kind of read! Angela Quarles is an up-and-coming contemporary romance writer to watch." — Lia Riley, author of the Off the Map and Hellions Angels series

"...a beautiful feel good romance..."
— Keeana with Bookalicious Babes Blog

ALSO BY ANGELA QUARLES

To Jilliene
Enjoy!

Earning it

Angela Quarles

ANGELA
QUARLES

Unsealed
ROOM PRESS

This is a work of fiction. Names, characters, places, and incidents either are the product of the author's imagination or are used fictitiously. Any resemblance to actual events, locales, or persons, living or dead, is purely coincidental, except where it is a matter of historical record.

To the men and women keeping Irish sports alive

A note about hurling and a short glossary

Luke and his teammates play an ancient Irish game called hurling, dubbed as the fastest game on grass. Players use sticks like hockey, but instead of a puck, they use a round ball similar to a baseball. Players can catch the round balls in their bare hands and hit them like a baseball, and ball speeds have been recorded as high as one hundred miles per hour. Needless to say, it can get rough on the field.

Hurling and Gaelic football are two Irish sports that are overseen by the Gaelic Athletic Association (GAA). But what makes it different than other national sports is that the GAA prohibits the players from earning a salary. So these players in Ireland—who are followed with the same level of fervor Americans follow their pro-sports players and soccer (football) fans worldwide follow their fave teams—are doing it solely for the love of the sport, not for the money. After a rough game, they go home to their day jobs.

Sliotar – the ball, pronounced "slitter"

Hurley – the stick, which is a bit fuller at the whacking end than a hockey stick

GAA – Gaelic Athletic Association, the governing body for the sport, which oversees hurling and its close cousin, Gaelic football.

1

```
ur 2 cold
```

I GLARE AT the four-month-old text, barely glancing at the bearded hipster bumping past me on the sidewalk. The sender? That'd be my ex. The hockey goalie who slapped away our year-long relationship with a text. Well, a series of texts over a five-minute span.

I'm killing time, and like someone who keeps picking, picking, picking at a scab, I'd pulled up those texts to stare at that last one. Cold?

Ambitious. Driven. Yes.

But cold?

I shove the phone into its pocket in my purse. I am *not* my parents. Thinking of those two fills me with a familiar but fuzzy unease.

A searing wave of fuck-that-asshole follows. He's still infecting my life—what I need is closure. I can't let that infection spill into my new life here in my old hometown. I yank the phone back out, resigned at this point to looking like an idiot to anyone who might be watching.

An article on Facebook from yesterday waves at me— hello, perfect revenge!

Tap, tap, tap. A quick search, a phone call, and…Yes.

I mash the end call icon on my Samsung and do a tee-hee dance on the sunny sidewalk. I sheepishly glance around to see who witnessed my little bout of enthusiasm on Sarasota's Main Street, but the locals and the few meandering tourists are preoccupied with their own lives this morning. Why should I care anyway, right?

Because thanks to my vengeance-driven donation, there's now a Madagascar hissing cockroach at the Bronx Zoo graced with the name Phil Stoddart.

It might be a placebo, but damn, it feels fantastic.

That task hasn't wasted enough time, so I pop under the barely cooler shade of one of the pin oaks lining the street and enter today's tasks in my app. It's my last day for errands before I start work with my new medical practice. Ha—look at me being all casual. *My* new *medical practice.*

Try first. Yesterday, seeing the nameplate next to my door—Dr. Rodgers—had brought goose bumps along my arms, making everything terrifyingly and excitingly *real.* I'm finally starting my career as a sports medicine doc. See, it's *that* life I can't wait to start after twelve grueling years of schooling, but instead, I'm five minutes early for a coffee date I'd rather not go on, much less be early to. So yeah, I'm stalling.

My high school best friend set me up with a colleague at her law firm. A lawyer? No, thanks—got enough of them growing up. (Read: my parents.) But since she's the only old friend I still want to hang with here, I succumbed. What's one morning?

All right. That's as much as I can reasonably stall. Now to face Rick the Lawyer, make small talk, and sip overpriced coffee. Maybe he'll surprise me. With the fresh reminder of Phil's opinion of me, maybe it'll be good to swim in the dating pool again. Live a little.

I dodge the sidewalk amblers and push through the door of the Mocha Cabana exactly one minute early. The rich scent of coffee and sweet pastries envelops me. Customers of all ages are bunched around the café-style tables. The population has definitely skewed younger since childhood. When I moved away, the realization that not everyone was seventy-plus years old was an eye-opener.

I do a quick scan—all I have to go on is that he's my age, he's got dark hair, and his name is Rick. And he's a lawyer.

I paste on a smile.

My gaze latches onto the man by the corner window, whose unnervingly masculine face is bisected by the fluctuating shadow of a nodding palm frond outside. The table in front of him is practically Lilliputian, he's so huge. He's the only man in the place matching Rick's description, though, and my heart does a tee-hee dance of its own. And I can tell, in that odd way that happens sometimes, that he knows I've arrived and is aware of me viscerally. That he's watching without watching, because the air between us has that crackly, weighty anticipation that triggers my sixth sense. This guy will have significance in my life, it says.

Combined with a rush of attraction? Not the reaction I want for a lawyer—or for anyone right now. Shit.

But Lordy, he must work out in his off hours. He's fit in a way you rarely see outside of movies and comic books. His hair is midnight black, and if it wasn't just past his ears, I'd totally peg him for active military—but not in the way you might think. He doesn't have those all-American good looks honed into sharp cheekbones and jaw like you associate with Marines. No. It's in the posture, the confidence, the strength. He owns—dominates—the space around him.

He *has* sharp cheekbones, but they're not part of an overall shiny, do-gooder package. Instead, they're combined with an olive skin tone, five-o'clock shadow, and a commanding nose that all adds up to Devastating.

Yipes, this easily-six-foot-two stack of hunky muscle is a lawyer and—I swallow—my blind date.

Pulse stupidly racing and that weighty awareness tingling up my back, I shuffle into line to order my café mocha. Deep breath. Live a little, I remind myself.

Swim in the dating pool? Now I want to splash in it, and I can't tell if it's because I want to cause a distraction or revel in the sheer *fun*.

One thing I *do* know—this reaction is *so* not like me.

○

LUKE

YEAH, I SAW her come in. Yeah, it's now forty-two seconds past my self-allotted time for staying in this frou-frou place. But can you blame a guy? The curvy brunette in the red dress snagged my attention as soon as she strolled in. The space around her seems less...murky.

That's not quite right. As a Navy SEAL, details are *always* dialed in, so it's not that my surroundings shifted from fuzzy to sharp. The clouds didn't part and reveal her in full sunshine or any of that crap. No. But the details are usually flat. Now it's as if she makes the space more...vibrant. 3D.

She doesn't see me at first, so I steal a moment and let my gaze linger. My hands flex—her trim but lush figure makes me want to trace all those curves. Grip her hips. Such a contrast to her glossy hair pulled into a reserved bun at the nape of her neck, which screams *take me seriously*. The red liquid of her dress hugs those grippable curves, teasing, promising. The Florida sun bathes her gorgeous face in warm light.

Shit. I'm getting downright poetic.

I press two fingers to my pulse. Cuz this shit isn't normal.

I still, my instincts fully engaged, because something about her is familiar, but I can't zero in on what. And now it's ninety seconds past my time, and I *should* be dumping this joke of a coffee and getting on with my day, but, yeah, the brunette. Maybe she's getting her order to-go, and I can see her on the way out. Okay, see her fine ass, cuz she's gotta have one, right?

And that's why I'm thrown off guard. Something else that's not normal. A swath of red fills my peripheral vision, scant inches from my face, and I know without looking up it's her. A coconut scent wafts over me. Wafts? Did I just use the word *waft?*

A delicate throat clears, and an intriguing voice says tentatively, "Rick?"

I look up, ready to correct her. Lucky Rick.

But I pause. And go very, very still.

Holy. Shit. It's Pepper Rodgers from high school. Pepper of the hormone-fueled teenage fantasies. Pepper the ever-optimistic. Pepper whom I totally humiliated at the science fair senior year. I'd call her the one who got away, but I never had her.

Her brown eyes don't flash with recognition.

Can't fault her. I'm not the shuffling beanpole with braces and acne she knew in high school.

Suddenly, I don't want to correct her and lose my opportunity to be around her for the next few minutes she might grant me. Cuz she wouldn't want to talk to Luke Haas—or Haashole as she dubbed me—but she obviously wants to talk to this Rick person.

And doesn't know who he is.

2

I survey the busy café. Completely unnecessary—no one has come in around my age and hair color. While I don't know any of the customers, most are familiar by sight. Sarasota's a small town when it gets right down to it. And during the summer? Most are local. In the winter, it's different—our population swells twenty percent with all the tin can tourists and snowbirds burrowing down here to escape the cold.

All the while, Pepper's puzzled gaze is a subtle pressure, waiting for me to make a decision and speak.

I lock eyes with her and, God help me, smile. No affirmation or denial, but a gesture that could be misinterpreted. Not proud of it, but…fuck. My gut whispers that this is a stolen moment, and I want to be that thief. Badly.

Besides, she doesn't live here anymore. Hasn't since we graduated twelve years ago. Normally, my life operates within that dangerous slice defined by the phrase "margin for error," and I do my damnedest to keep that margin slim. Keeping it slim and trim is the only way I've gotten anywhere in life.

This here? It's outside the parameters of slim margin for error, but that's how bad I want this.

I can be Rick for a morning. Be someone other than

8

an expensively well-trained shell posing as human. Alleviate the monotony of my life. For a brief moment. Until she recognizes me. The odds are damn high it'll only be a moment—the subterfuge will be over quickly if this is a business meeting.

So, yeah, I curve my lips, and am rewarded by the most stunning, hits-me-in-the-solar-plexus smile. I've never received any of her smiles, and damn if I don't want it to be the first of many I'd catalog. Note the time and date. The cause and effect. Because this smile achieves what little else does—penetrates through the gray and lights me up with color. Because this smile transforms her face from a put-together, beautiful brunette, to a gorgeous but personable woman. And fuck, there's the beauty mark on her right temple that I remember vividly. Vividly because it drove me crazy. Makes no sense, but the vision of a lick on that spot as step one in the exploration of her whole body was my teenage wank material.

Aaaand apparently it still does it for me. Huh.

She sticks out her hand, and the move, while confident-looking, has an overlay of nervous bravado. "Hi, so nice to meet you! I'm Pepper, but I guess you figured that out."

Her voice has changed since high school—more confident and mature. No nonsense, yet its tones seep into me, warming me. Her outstretched hand beckons, and—still floored I'm going with this new plan—I stand and slide my palm against hers, completely engulfing her small hand. Her skin sears mine, warm and silky, a one-two lust combo. A jolt of arousal spikes through me. Another surprise for the day. I'm racking the fuckers up like kill points ever since she walked in. Before I look like a complete ape-man, I grasp her hand and shake, a firm one that signals she has my respect.

Her laugh has an edge—another indicator she's nervous. She slips into the opposite seat in a graceful twist, and I follow suit. She's all curves, right in front of me. Vibrant. Anxious. Pepper.

That anxious-vibrant combo punches me—I'm not worth

that much mental anxiety. I stop myself from reaching out to clasp her hand in some kind of primitive protective gesture. I want to soothe her. No doubt exists that I've affected her. Good. Sucks to be the only one.

I need more background intel, so I sit back and risk keeping quiet. Occupy my stolen moment for as long as I can. She doesn't disappoint.

"Can you believe Tricia?" She sets down her red coffee mug and straightens her spoon on the saucer, the rattle and clink barely audible in the noise of the café. Did I mention that everything is red here? Dealing with all this relentless red is one of the reasons I come here. I'm waiting for the sheer solid front of it to penetrate and normalize everything, but it hasn't yet.

"Unbelievable," I answer. A safe reaction to whatever Tricia's done.

She angles forward, her head tilting almost in apology. "This is my first blind date, so you'll have to forgive me."

Ah. A blind date. Now that I know the situation, I adjust to the new intel, but then her thumb rubs up and down the handle of her mug. Of course, I transfer the action to someplace my mind has no business going.

I clear my throat and shift in my seat, leaning forward. "Mine too. We're both blind date virgins then." Jesus, that sounded cheesy. But she takes it in stride. "How much did Tricia tell you?"

The odds are looking better that I can stretch the moment. Be Rick.

"Nothing except, you know"—she waves a hand at me—"how you look. I know you're a partner in her law firm." At that, her eyes flare with panic—odd. It's gone just as fast. Since I know fuck all about law, I'll need to keep our conversation away from work. If I don't ask her about her job, maybe she won't ask about mine.

She bites her lip. Which acts like a fucking missile, shooting another bolt of lust through me. Down, boy.

I absolutely can*not* go there. Not with her.

But the space between us is sexually charged, as if it has a weight of its own and is simultaneously pushing against us and pulling us toward each other. The sensation's a new one.

Wait. No. It's exactly how it was in high school. When that sensation penetrated and confused my puny adolescent, hormone-addled brain into being a dipshit to her. As if I knew it meant something, and I needed to take action, but I had no fucking clue and just, yeah, did stupid shit.

So. My plan is clear. Be a new person. Be this Rick the Lawyer. And talk to the only woman who's ever made me feel any kind of spark outside of combat for the space of this coffee date. Best case scenario, I get to be outside my skin—free to be whatever the hell I want. Worst case—she recognizes me as we chat. She'll be pissed, call me an asshole, but it won't be anything she hasn't called me in the past, so… Win/Win?

Pepper

HOLY YUMMY PRESENCE, Batman. I have no words, which is unusual for me, to be honest. I don't want him to shatter the gorgeous-man illusion with law talk, so the blip in my brain is me scrambling for another conversational topic. I'd planned to coast through this date by asking him about his job and letting him rattle on, because that's what guys seem to do best—talk about themselves. Especially on first dates. So I've heard.

I wrap my hands around my mug, letting the warmth ground me. I blow into it to stall. My brain isn't helped out by the zing I feel being this close to him. He's the definition of sex on a stick. Normally, I don't even say stuff like that, but I heard it on some show and it pops, all unwelcome, into my brain. And that's a little too overwhelming for me, so…

"Um, are you new in town?"

No judging. I've gotta start somewhere, and it's obvious he's not going to take the plunge. My voice comes out a little thready, but I put on a brave face.

He leans back, and the movement sends a scent my way. *His* scent. And of course it's intoxicating. Manly. Sex-on-a-stupid-stick manly. No doubt he received more than his share of pheromones when he was made. I do *not* lean forward to keep it in range.

Okay, I do.

To cover my action, I prop my chin on my hand and wait for his response like I'm all calm, but really I'm like a dog whose rump hits the floor in record speed, tail thumping madly, waiting for my treat—his voice. I've only gotten four sentences out of him so far, but those four sentences?

Sexy. Well, not the sentences themselves, but the voice that carries them. Deep, rumbling, self-assured.

Sexy.

Jeez, my brain is stuck on that word. I do my best to feign polite interest instead of oh-my-God-can-you-just-sit-there-and-be-any-more-sexy?

All right. That word's now banned from my vocabulary. I'd like to get through this blind date with dignity, thank you very much. Especially since this type of over-the-top reaction is new, like a feverish infection.

"Moved here from Virginia Beach about two years ago." His voice prickles over my skin, fills me. Burrows into some lonely part of me I didn't know was there. And then kicks my heart rate into a greater pace, because I absolutely do *not* know how to handle the attraction I'm feeling for this stranger. This can't be normal, can it?

I bite off a piece of chocolate croissant and lick the crumbs from my lips.

"And you?" He takes a sip of coffee and looks at me over the rim, his eyes carrying a knowing kind of weight to them. God. He can tell I have the hots for him.

I stop myself. Normally, I'd feel like the potato salad

caught thinking it was a fancy *amuse-bouche* to have a chance with someone like him. But now I'm like, screw it. So I think he's hot and he knows it. Is that a crime?

I moved back to my hometown because I want to start fresh. Be the new me I put on hold for twelve mind-numbing, sleep-deprived years. And the new me is totally fine with a hot guy knowing I find him attractive. Might be good to see where this goes. New town. New fling. New not-cold me.

Take that, Phil.

But I'm bungling it already, because that was a stupid-long pause. God—it's as if I have little dating experience. Haha. That's me being sarcastic, because that's exactly what this is. I'm twenty-nine, but I might as well be eighteen.

The sad truth is—I poured all of my twenties into school. Phil was my first and only real relationship, and that came about because it unfolded with little effort on my part—he was a patient—and because I *thought* that finally reaching the fellowship stage of my schooling meant I could create time for a relationship. Boy, had that been an epic miscalculation.

And now, I've paused even loooonger.

As if to punctuate the ridiculous silence, the frothing machine behind me chooses now to *scroooosh* overloud and overlong. I wait until it's done and say, "I grew up here." I take a sip of my café mocha, grateful to have something to do with my hands—they're like fluttery, alien things with no direction.

His gaze hasn't left mine, and I resist shifting in my seat. "Must've been nice, growing up near such beautiful beaches."

"Sure," I say, because that's what everyone expects, but honestly, it wasn't. I hated the whole smearing down with lotion and baking in the sun thing. Classmates filled my yearbooks with snide remarks about my pale state. *Get a tan, girl* was my fave of the lot. "But tell me about Virginia Beach. I've never been."

He leans forward, takes the bait—thank God—and regales me with stories about his buddies there, their pranks, his favorite spots, but all the while I'm thinking our conversation is really about something else.

I do get a vivid picture of the Virginia Beach he knows, and I want to visit. See these places. With him.

This is nuts.

It's just…he's so deliciously self-assured, as if he's in complete control of himself and whatever situation befalls him, and the thought sends a thrill through me. He's so out of my league, but a girl can pretend. It's not that I think I'm pond scum or something, but I'm average in the looks department and my limited dating experience places him in the unattainable sphere.

Unease worms its way into my newfound resolve to live a little. Seeing his control—his ease and charm—highlights how different we are. We might both be self-assured business professionals, but only for *him* does it carry over into his dating life. I lack that. And I'm surprised to find this bothers me. Not about him. God no. But about me.

I polish off my chocolate croissant, trying to enjoy its sweet buttery flavor as I listen to him and struggle with what to think. What to do.

His words and my words and our breaths are combining across this café table in this corner coffee shop, and I feel as if there are other presences here with us: my nerves, for one; a weighty, breathless expectation; potential.

However, as the minutes pass and conversations and customers ebb and flow around us, it no longer *feels* as if he's out of my league. We just click, and it seems so completely natural to be here talking. With him.

For instance, how weird is it that we both visited Nuremberg the same year, but a month apart?

"*Sprechen Sie Deutsch?*" he asks, with a challenging eyebrow lift.

"*Ja,*" I answer, but my German's rusty, and I say so in German. I continue in English, "It was a stop on a short tour of Southern Germany before I started my spring semester abroad in Munich. Stayed at the coolest youth hostel, a converted castle."

He chuckles, a sound that drops into that weighty

expectation and sizzles along my nerves. "I stayed there too."

See? *Click*. Fate. I shift forward in my seat. "It was raining when I got there, so I didn't get to appreciate it at first, but I met two Canadians—a brother and sister—and we had a great time holed up in our room."

He nods along. "More people should travel abroad, if they're able. We're so isolated here. Most Americans don't get how weird it is that we can travel for hours and hours and still speak the same language."

Which leads to a discussion on the merits of experiencing other cultures. Somewhere in that time, a barista clears away our dishes. Before I know it, a whole hour has disappeared, and we've been talking, laughing, sharing, and I honestly can't remember the last time I felt so free with someone. A whole hour in which he hasn't once glanced at his watch as if he can't wait for an excuse to leave my presence.

A whole hour which has been an exercise in restraint. Restraint from reaching out and touching the skin on the back of his hand, feeling the hairs brush against my palm. Restraint from running my fingers up his muscled forearm, because I totally want to feel his strength whisper across my skin. Restraint from asking, are you for real?

Restraint from leaning in and letting his warrior-like body shelter me. Which is screwed up because I don't need sheltering. But I get the vibe that if I had a problem, he'd know how to fix it. And he'd want to.

The realization that our date is close to over washes through me and leaves behind a jittery, panicky residue. It's the only reason I can explain my next words, "Let's have sex."

I clap a hand over my mouth, and I know my eyes have about bugged out of my head. "Holy shit," I whisper. My heart's pounding as if it's going what-the-hell? But I actually wait for a response, because it turns out, I was kind of serious. Actually, I totally am.

Wow.

I've got some she-balls, and I'm loving it. The new me.

Apparently he is too, because his eyes grow dark, hooded,

and the air shifts between us, growing even more charged. It's like—we've clicked so well, uncovering so much common ground between us, that it's left a vacuum which demands to be filled by a physical connection. To even the balance. To shore up the gains we made.

Except. That uneasiness returns and knocks around in my stomach. I have no time for the emotional investment a relationship takes. Yeah, I'm starting my new-me phase of my life, but I'm not ready to make time for a relationship. And then I have to laugh at myself for thinking so far ahead, but I can't help it. It's hard-wired. I miscalculated during my fellowship and indulged in a relationship with Phil. I can't risk that again. I need to solidify my base here before I can…expand.

But a fling? That might be exactly what I need to prove to myself I'm not cold. And to be upfront about this, I say, "This'll just be sex. No strings. Afterward? We part ways."

That last bit was hard to say, because everything in me aches to explore more with this man, but I…can't. Too much is on the line professionally. I'm already starting at the practice on shaky ground.

So if this is all I can have with him? Yeah, I want the sex too.

Then we'll never see each other again.

I could have kept quiet. Supposedly, guys don't care—they'd never say no to sex—but I always thought that truism was a bit too pat. Since I'm basically using him to get practice and gain some much-needed experience, I need to be honest. Especially because it feels as if we've made a connection.

He leans forward, his elbows propping on the table. His biceps bunch, and his whole body shudders with a slight tension.

Shit. Have I totally misread him? Us? Will the one time I say something bold and daring—the one time I take ownership of something I want sexually, the one time I decide to live a little—be the time I get shot down?

An internal struggle plays out in the depths of his green

eyes. Did I mention they're green? Well, they are. A rich, layered kind of green that surprisingly makes me want to curl up and stare into them. All day.

He still hasn't uttered a word.

You know what? If I'm going to channel a sex vixen today, I need to own it.

Slowly, I stand and hold his gaze. Then I turn and stroll toward the door as if I know what the hell I'm doing. As if I'm super confident he's going to follow me. As if I've totally done this before.

A chair scrapes.

OMG.

My thighs are shaky. I sure hope it's not ruining the saunter I'm going for. Then, his warm presence is behind me, and a delicious shiver races down my spine. And that's before his hand presses against the small of my back, sending a dose of heat to my core.

OMG. This is so happening.

LUKE

FUUUUCK.

I'm leaning forward holding the café door open for Pepper, and I'm so close I can feel her warmth, see the short hairs that have escaped the no-nonsense bun to soften the line of her creamy neck. Begging me to lick, to taste her skin. To flick and tease the small hairs and nibble my way up to…

Lust burns through me, making it hard to think.

And I need to *think*, dammit.

But I'm here and holding the door open precisely because each justification I made to steal more time out of this moment has been like a domino, click-click-clicking its inevitable path down and away—out of my control. I can stop this forward momentum. I can stop and say…

Pepper, I'm Luke from high school, the one you hate, but can we forget all that and keep…connecting? I actually didn't do what you think I did…

Pepper, we can't do this because…

We walk down the sunlit sidewalk, my hand warming at the small of her back and…no words come out. She's leading, I'm following, and… Yeah. She's in charge. Which is hot. And I'm along for the ride, however that ride plays out. The little mind embodied in my cock perks up again, imagining all the "riding" we can do.

No. That's not the point. The point is… The fucking point is…

The point is, she's in charge, and she wants this. And I do too. And she's set the parameters of the engagement. One time only. And maybe she'll chicken out and change her mind before we get there…

My breath shudders, fighting against the sudden, constrictive weight on my chest.

Fuck, I'm the asshole she believes me to be because I can't back away from this.

Yeah, the justifications are coming swift and hard, detonating like mortar shells, one after another against my rational mind. But one justification eclipses all—we're never seeing each other again.

3

AT RICK'S APARTMENT complex, a naked bulb illuminates a clean but bare stairwell painted a cool blue. All is hushed anticipation except for our breaths and the scrape of our shoes as we take one step, and then another. I'm acutely aware of my surroundings, especially of the man behind me. But I'm not scared.

No, instead I'm wound up for a completely different reason. Soon I'll be feeling him against me. Feeling his strength. And I'm...eager. Eager to taste his skin, eager to learn what turns him on, eager to explore this sizzling chemistry flaring between us. Because it's just so unusual for me. And it could be my one chance. Phil didn't get me worked up like this. Guys have flirted with me in the past, but it just...never did anything for me. Deep down, I think the reason Phil's text bothered me so much was because I feared it was true.

We reach the first landing, and he palms the small of my back again, the solid tips of his fingers settling into the dip along my spine, steady and sure. A shudder of anticipation and heat starts at the point of contact and fans outward. We've barely talked since leaving the coffee shop. In fact, all that was said was on his part.

His words, like velvet in my ear but dark with sensual promise, "My apartment's a block away," and I just nodded like that eager puppy.

God. This is really happening.

I'm having sex with someone I just met. Before lunchtime.

And I'm oddly fine with this.

I take the next step, and he follows more closely now, his hunky presence behind me like a heady, sensual pressure. His intoxicating scent already making my stomach flutter.

His warm breath brushes my ear, and I shiver.

"You sure about this, sweetheart?"

His voice is infused with a touch of worry, which totally checks another box in his pro column.

"Yes," I whisper, still trying my damnedest to channel this new sex vixen in me. And since a sex vixen wouldn't stop there, I reach down and stroke my hand down his muscular thigh. Which…might not be that sexy, but dammit, to me this is radical.

Through his suede-soft jeans, his taut muscles tense under my palm, and he growls in my ear. I clench. I friggin' clench, which I've never done in my life. How pathetic. Obviously, this lack is something vital I need to fix.

At his door, he yanks me into the sheltering circle of his arm, my back flush against him, his body curled around me. For some reason, being so definitively in his personal space—his inner circle—feels more intimate than anything I've done in the past. My hand flexes on his thigh, itching to move up and squeeze the powerful biceps which fill my left-side vision. But I resist. Yeah, just call me Miss Self Control.

He fishes out his key from his jeans pocket, the action curving his hips into me and pressing his heavy erection against the top curve of my ass. I tremble, and heat pulses through my veins.

The door swings inward, and he edges us forward. I snatch a glimpse of bare white walls, sparse furniture, and a general lack of clutter, when I'm spun around and he sandwiches me against the now-closed door.

Our heightened breaths are all I can hear. His hard body is stretched against mine, tensed, and arousal spikes through me, a searing heat all along my skin. That was…fucking hot. Do I want to have sex against a door? Yes. Yes, I do.

He leans forward, his face mere inches from mine, his gaze searching, but his mouth doesn't crash into mine like I expect. Instead, he says, "Listen." His liquid voice steals over me, mixing with my desire and ratcheting it higher. "That door's unlocked. You initiated, yes. But that doesn't mean you can't change your mind. Understand?"

I shiver again, because damn, the heat and control radiating from him envelops me in his protective zone. And his concern soothes any last minute anxiety that's trying its damnedest to knock sense into me. I appreciate the check-in, don't get me wrong, but I'm eager to explore this.

A strange noise—half growl, half groan—rumbles from his chest. "You asked, you're in charge, but I also want. Fuck, do I want."

He tracks his gaze down my body and back up, taking in the rise and fall of my breasts. Which are practically begging all on their own for his touch. His eyes lock with mine, and the want there sends another bolt of need through me, because—holy cow—this huge, hotter-than-sin man wants me. *Wants* me.

I nod. It's all I'm capable of. That, and the hand I'd put on his thigh earlier. Yeah, I'm a regular sex vixen, all right.

I grab the neckline of his gray T-shirt and yank him the rest of the way across the sliver of charged space still between us. Somehow our foreheads or noses don't crash together from the force of my tug, but our mouths do, and we both take, take, take, as if we've been waiting all our lives to do just this. He nudges me back into the door with his hips, and his strong hands cup my jaw and cheeks as if I'm a delicate creature.

But his kisses aren't delicate. Not at all. His tongue strokes mine, and that taste punches my sensual fever higher. I brush my hands up to his muscled shoulders and do a half-grab of his neck, half-grab of his hair.

He hisses and breaks our kiss, his eyes closing.

"I'm sooo going to hell," he mutters.

Before I can think or ask what he means, he hikes me up as if I'm some lightweight and presses his hard cock against my clit, one of the metal buttons of his Levi 501s pushing right against… Oh shit, yes. I whip my legs around his waist. Apparently, I'm channeling a gymnast now too.

He trails his hypnotic mouth across my jaw and down my neck. And that delicious weight is just…pressed there. Driving me wild. I squirm against him to relieve the building pressure, and, oh Jesus, it winds me tighter and tighter.

He growls and thrusts his hips, picking up on the rhythm I crave. Need. And then I'm panting, pulling his hair, grinding against him as if he's my own personal sex toy, looking up at his pebbly ceiling, and thinking, holy shit, this is the hottest thing I've ever experienced. The tension is coiling and building inside me, desperate, feverish.

And just like that, I shatter.

Didn't I say I needed to get out more?

Because, yeah, I just came against a door by grinding on a guy. Fully clothed.

Heat rushes up my skin, my legs and arms tightening around him as I ride out my climax, trembling.

"Fuck, that was hot," he grits out. He lifts his head and glances behind him, the tension and control obviously fighting for dominance in his rigidly taut muscles, the strain around his mouth and eyes. "Not here."

He spins around with me still clinging to him. But since my muscles feel gooey, he must be the one holding me in place.

"Bedroom. Back there."

Apparently, he's also reduced to simple statements. I cinch my noodle arms around his neck as best I can, and his mouth slants against mine, his breaths and lips frantic, needy. Urgent.

He heads for his bedroom, his strides long and purposeful

and powerful, the movement massaging his cock against my core. I'm still all languid and limp from my release, but this sparks a new flare of desire. We pass the breakfast bar facing his galley kitchen, and his steps slow. He stops and places his forehead against mine, pulling in a deep breath and slowly letting it out. Then again.

What the—?

He pushes aside a wooden stool with his foot, crashing it to the floor. My butt hits the countertop, and his hands are grazing up my thighs, bunching my red sundress up against my hips. The soft cotton teases across my now sensitized skin. I'm totally on board, because I can't wait either. I want him inside me.

Shit. I'd chosen plain white boy shorts in defiance of this date. A statement that I knew it wouldn't go anywhere. Minus one for me in the sex vixen role. But he doesn't seem to mind. His devastating eyes are hooded, and he skims his hands farther up, cupping my ass. The possessive grip makes me shiver.

He tugs me toward him—my ass sliding smoothly across the surface—and traces a hand down my neck. "Just one more taste," he rumbles.

I love that he can't wait until we get to his room. His lips brush mine, gently this time, but apparently that's just too damn slow for me because I'm gripping the back of his head and increasing the urgency of the kiss. All of the post-orgasmic lusciousness has transmuted into a growing need for him.

He breaks away on a sharp inhale, eyes closing. "Shit, sweetheart."

It's endearing he calls me that when it's just sex, but I'm again confused by the slow-down.

My question is answered with his next words. "We can…" He clears his throat. "We can still end this now if you want. You got off…"

Does he not want…? I glance down. No. I can see the evidence that he very much wants to continue.

I shake my head. "I want this. I need this." And I do.

I've already learned so much about myself this afternoon, with him, and somehow I feel as if this is my one chance to explore this new side of me—try it on for practice until I'm ready to implement it in my life.

I can see he's still hesitant.

"Whatever noble ideas you've got pinging around in there, stop. I want this. I want you. Now." I take another breath. Own it, own it, own it. Now I'm the one who grabs his ass possessively. "Please." I follow up with a nibble on his ear lobe.

On a curse, he whips his wallet from his back pocket and tosses it onto the counter, the rippling and flexing of his muscles as he moves, a thing of beauty. His wallet spins and thumps against my hip. His hands fly to his waist, and he's tugging up the hem of his T-shirt and unbuttoning his jeans. Triumph surges through me, swift and powerful. I glimpse rock-hard abs and a sprinkling of hair arrowing down, and my pulse beats hard in my neck—I can *feel* it—and I sway a little bit at the need that's clawing up inside me. Need for this man. Right now.

And then I still. Whoa.

He's a commando guy.

His cock is thick, long, and hard, pushing up his T-shirt. I need to touch. I stretch out my fingers—they're trembling—and drag a fingertip across the swollen head. The soft cotton of his shirt, warm from being next to his skin, brushes the backs of my fingers. He shudders, and his erection jerks slightly away. I stroke down the backside and wrap my fingers around his thickness. His heat pulses beneath my palm, warming my skin. Firm, smooth, hot.

Totally hot.

He groans and snatches his wallet. Before I can even blink, he has a condom whipped out and rolled on, and now he's shoving aside my panties. He takes a moment to stroke a blunt fingertip through my slick folds, but it's friggin' obvious I'm so ready for him.

He possessively palms my ass again, but this time he strokes into me in one swift thrust. Oh God. He's so thick and hard, and it's been a long, long time for me, so he's not all the way in. But already I feel so, so full of him, his wide girth a searingly luscious intrusion. More.

I whip my legs around his hips and dig my heels into his butt. He grunts—a long, drawn-out one that could pass for a groan—and its timbre vibrates through me *down there*.

His mouth crashes into mine, and a hand trails up my waist and cups a breast as he slowly pulls out. God, the drag of his cock away from me makes me even more desperate, even though I know he'll be back. But it can't be soon enough. I press my heels into him again, urging him back inside, just barely restraining from beating against his ass in my jittery, impatient anticipation. He slams back into me. Fully seated. Fully filling me.

We both still. And shudder. *Holy shit. He's huge.*

"Thanks," he grunts.

Mortification that I voiced that out loud burns up my skin, but it can't compare to the urgency racing through my blood, pinging against me for release, starting from where he fills me so deliciously. I don't care anymore. I just want him to fuck me. *Fuck me hard.*

"I plan to," he drawls.

Good God. I'm hopeless, but it doesn't matter because he's pounding into me, his generous, rigid length relentless as it sears into me over and over, our greedy mouths kissing any surface we can reach.

Our breathy pants and needy hands are everywhere. We're practically tearing each other apart in our desperation. Both of us chasing the orgasm. One of my high heels flings across the room, landing with a smack.

He growls against my neck, "God, please tell me you're—"

At the same time I gasp, "I'm about to come!"

A tiny part of me is sitting in a corner—round-eyed and mouth agape—that I'm now a talker during sex. A dirty talker.

Then the orgasm that's been hurtling toward me bursts inside.

Wow. Guess I'm a screamer too.

4

Pepper

My Volvo's tires scrunch over gravel as I pull in next to an overabundance of trucks, all clustered in packs under the shade cast by the live oaks lining the parking lot. I grab my field kit and car blanket and walk fast enough across the lot to reach the next patch of shade, but not so fast to work up a sweat. The Spanish moss dangling from the trees hangs like festive lace in the still but sultry air.

At the gate in the chain link fence bordering the soccer fields, I transfer the bag to my left hand and squeeze through. Shouts beyond the copse of trees ahead indicate which direction I need to steer toward.

The grass is squishy-wet from an afternoon sun shower, here and gone before you can even think of getting an umbrella, but leaving behind a languid mugginess. Nothing can diffuse my happiness, though. My body is deliciously sore from all the sexing yesterday, and I giggle just thinking that I can actually make such a statement. A newfound power, and heat, rushes through me, lending my steps a certain perkiness.

Rick and I did make it to his bed, where we tried out moves horizontally and other ways. Damn, that lawyer knew his way around the sack. And that lawyer has a hidden wild side—I discovered intricate tattoos along his left arm, which I found surprisingly hot.

It was a new side of me. And I love it.

Hallelujah, I'm *not* cold. I'm not my parents. I'd just been asleep for a long time, sexually. At one point with Rick, my stomach growled. He launched out of bed and pulled me into the kitchen, where he chopped up veggies, threw some meat in a pan, and whipped up a late lunch as if it was nothing.

Part of me regrets my deal with him, but I'm squeezing that part to a pulp. The last thing I need right now as I embark on my career—finally—is a relationship. The older doctors in my practice are definitely wary of my age and judgment. You could practically see the words hanging above their heads like comic book thought bubbles—*She's so young. Can she be professional? Should we risk it? What if she gets married? Will she again write prescriptions cavalierly?*—popping up over their heads as they looked at each other and then back at me during the initial interview. Plus, I'm only a locum, filling in for a Dr. Tekin while he's on medical leave. They're using this as an opportunity to test me out before they expand their practice next year.

The emotional rollercoaster of my residency taught me how to maintain a delicate balance of calm detachment, and even the mild, textbook relationship with Phil had ruffled that hard-won veneer. In the end, it hadn't even been worth the trouble, while it also got me into so much trouble. So with someone like Rick? Who already made me feel so much? I could lose my compass before I've even established my bearings here.

Up ahead, I see my new patients—a fit bunch of guys hitting a white ball around a soccer field with what looks like a pregnant hockey stick. Another reason my happy glow can't be dimmed? This hurling team represents my first consultation as a bona fide doctor. It's going to go great, despite the fact that the guy who poured Diet Coke down my winning science fair project will be there. Luke Haas. Or Haashole, as I called him. Yeah, I noticed that name on the roster passed along to our office.

Yes. Yesterday's fling was just what the doctor ordered. I know, bad pun. But the fling proved something to me, and now I can start my new life in my old hometown looking forward instead of backward, ready to unleash my not-cold self when I'm ready and able. To indulge now would be irresponsible.

LUKE

I'M LATE, AND I don't do late. I don't do mistakes either. Ever. And taking Pepper home had been a mistake.

Yesterday, as it was happening, I somehow rationalized all of it, but the reality of exactly how much I fucked up slammed into me as soon as I walked her back to the coffee shop and kissed her goodbye. Yeah, I'd followed her lead. But she didn't have all the facts.

It wasn't right.

Well, the sex was right. More than right. Which makes this all wrong. So wrong.

As Shepherd Book in *Firefly* would say, I'm going to the special hell.

I pull sharply into a parking spot and yank up on the hand brake.

I'm gonna come clean, though. Find her, call her, and fess up. Yeah, she'll never want to speak to me again, but I knew that going in, didn't I? Dumb fucker that I am, I thought it'd be worth it just to spend time with her without her seeing me as an asshole. And then, good God, when she leaned forward and said in her sex kitten voice, "Let's have sex," I was a goner. A missile shot out of the rocket launcher of inevitability.

And now I have a goddamn boner.

I slam my door shut next to a blue Volvo that looks out of place, grab my gear from the back, and stride toward the gate and the gap in the trees ahead. Beyond is the clear field where our team practices.

Yeah, I'm gonna come clean, but first I have to find her. I'd spent the rest of my evening after she left running searches and calling in a few favors. So far...nothing. But when I find her, then...then I'll...fuck, I don't know, but it needs to be on the John Cusack with boom box level.

Fuck, I can't face the guys with a hard-on. I palm and spin the *sliotar*, my fingertips brushing the soft white leather. The words in black font, "O'Neills All-Ireland," come into focus on every other spin.

My phone rings from my gym bag. I'd ignore it, especially since I'm late, but I'm expecting an important call. "Haas," I grunt out. Then silently curse myself for making such a non-civvie greeting. "This is Luke Haas."

The sponsorship liaison with Langfield Corporation chirps across the connection, and I sift through her spiel, waiting for the magic words that'll earn my spot on the team. It's the call I've been waiting for all week. And then she says them— "...and so we're budgeting sponsorship funds this year. I'll have the contract pulled up and sent over. Honestly, I thought you were crazy proposing this. Hurling? But it turns out the [CEO] is totally fascinated with anything Irish, so..."

Yeah, not an accident. I'd drawn up a spreadsheet of all the major corporations in Sarasota and meticulously researched the interests of their [CEO]s. A longshot, but the research paid off upon discovering Scott Langfield is a frustrated Celtic scholar. It's amazing what you can discover on Google. Hadn't even needed to call in favors to find out this shit. From there it was a simple matter of drawing up a tactical plan.

I do a mental fist pump, but her next words yank me up short. "He's a little nervous with this being such a new sport here in the US. Corporate image and all. Can't afford lawsuits. So one of the requirements for securing the sponsorship is to submit all the players to a pre-participation physician examination to make sure everyone's fit, as well as a drug screening."

Cue eye roll. No problem there. We're all a fit bunch of guys. The physical demands of the sport require it. Besides, we'd all agreed to treat it like a pro sport—go big or go home, right? I memorize the rest of the details and hang up, eager to dispense with that formality. Whatever Mr. Langfield needs, I'll do.

Yes. Now my team can afford to send all fifteen of us to the division playoffs in Atlanta, and, if we win, to the national playoffs in Chicago. Most of us have our basic gear, but for some the travel, on top of the time off from work, was going to be hard to swing. This sponsorship can also pay for the flight from Ireland for the trainer we've wanted to put on the final polish.

While the national playoffs are still a ways off, we couldn't even think of going until we secured financing. And now we have it, after we meet his stipulations. Shouldn't be hard.

And for me, well, it just lets me extend this band of brothers thing for a bit longer.

I've no sooner hung up when it rings again, the ring tone announcing it's the private security firm I freelance with. Typically, I keep my season clear, so the fact that they're calling means it's important.

"Haas."

"Hate to tap you," Dennis says, "but we need a body with your skill set, and Frank is on another assignment."

"Hit me." When I discharged with honor from the Navy, since I didn't stay in long enough for a pension, I did what many with my special forces training do—hired myself out as a close protection officer. A bodyguard.

The rich snowbirds keep me booked solid during the winter—enough income to allow me the spring and summer off to do hurling.

"Slaine'll be here in a week for a show at the Van Wezel.

He's requested a bodyguard for his stay, which includes several high-profile fundraising dinners and other meet and greets. Before he arrives, we need you to run background checks on all the people he's scheduled to meet, scout the locations to assess the security and recommend upgrades, and supplement his usual entourage."

All pretty standard for a rock star of his stature. "Is he expecting any trouble?"

"Nothing outside of what he normally attracts, no."

I snort. Yeah, that dude always has some story in the papers. "When and how much?"

Because isn't that what it always comes down to? I memorize the details, and since both the timing and the money work for me, I agree. This new work moves another chip into play—I can use the money to front the expenses for the Irish trainer and the uniforms until the sponsorship money comes through. And if it doesn't, we're still covered. And I'll narrow the margin for error and prove my worth to the team.

Bodyguard work doesn't come close to the satisfaction I felt working as a SEAL, but like hurling, it keeps me fit, mentally and physically.

I never want to lose that edge.

I'd fought hard for that edge. The fear of failure had driven me through the training, and once I made the teams, the expectations placed on my performance honed it into a razor sharp, lethal edge.

Not bad for a poor, trailer-park kid.

But while the bodyguard gig utilizes some of my unique skill set, it lacks one major component—working as a team. No camaraderie. Enter—hurling.

PEPPER

WHAM!

In front of me, a player slams into another, who stumbles to the side, his hand striking the ground and saving him from a complete fall. I'd been leaning back on my hands, but I straighten, cross my legs on the blanket, and lean forward. I'd heard of hurling but had never seen it played. The rules seem whacked, but my first impression is that it's a rougher, faster version of lacrosse, with a mash-up of baseball, volleyball, field hockey, and rugby to add to the what-the-hell confusion.

And aside from the minimal lacrosse-style helmets, none of them wear protective gear. Not even shin guards. The testosterone permeates the humid air so thickly, I can almost taste it. None of them appear to be my science fair nemesis, but I can't get a closer look from where I sit. I know which one it *isn't*—I'd introduced myself to the captain when I arrived, letting him know what I needed to accomplish today.

I count fourteen instead of the fifteen I was told to expect, but then a straggler comes from the parking lot, his steps sure and long.

He taps a small white ball up, over and over, on the end of his stick, but I sense he's not showing off, but rather warming up before he enters the fray. Like the others, he has a helmet on, but his stride completely owns the space around him.

Then I catch myself—what's wrong with me? Did my completely out-of-character actions yesterday open me to finding men desirable everywhere I look? No doubt exists in my mind, though, that Rick awakened me in a way I didn't know needed awakening.

And then he gets closer, and my breath just ups and leaves. It's *him*.
Rick.
My hot-as-hell fling is *here*. My back straightens, and my

palms break out in a totally unfeminine sweat. Everything switches from the Simple column to Complicated.

Oh shit. He drops his gym bag behind the goal post and hustles to the others, joining them in their drills.

Panic has my stomach all scrambled. A fling. This was supposed to be a *fling*. And while, yes, I'd really, really, *really* love to see where things might lead, I know myself and I *have* to establish my career as a doctor first.

I'd already been having a hard time not slipping a note under Rick's door. I kept repeating, *be responsible*, whenever that temptation gripped me.

But now? Out of the question. He's a patient, and I can't cross that doctor-patient line again.

I'm mesmerized watching him play, though. Sure, I'd gotten an up-close-and-personal tour of the abs gracing his torso, but good God, seeing him move through the drills, using his body as an athletic machine, is spellbinding on a whole 'nother level. No doubt about it, his body is meant to be seen moving. There's also a bit of freedom in observing him from a distance, in the privacy of my…er, blanket, without him being aware. Jeez, I sound like a creeper. But it's also helping me detach back into work mode.

That fascination of seeing the human body work as an athletic machine is precisely why I love what I do—helping athletes efficiently and safely use their strength and skills. And helping them heal when injured. I'm a bit of a dork about it actually.

Soon enough, the captain blows a whistle, and the players stop and beeline for the nearby table lined with water jugs.

After they quickly hydrate, the captain heads my way with Rick and the rest of the team. I stand because I want to be cool and professional when they greet me, which is a bit difficult, I admit, when my heart is beating so hard I fear it's going to punch through my ribcage. My lady parts have also received the signal, and I shiver with anticipation and longing.

I wasn't supposed to see him again. He's now my patient.

But as they approach, Rick catches sight of me and his stride slows. I guess he's not looking forward to seeing me, and that hurts, even though I knew it was just a fling. Which was *my* decision, I remind myself.

I snap open my clipboard, ruthlessly shunting aside this unreasonable pain. When dignity is at risk, take refuge in work, right? And since facing my science fair nemesis might be the distraction I need, I call out, "Luke Haas," and hold out a medical questionnaire, the paper listlessly flapping in a mild breeze.

Rick takes a hesitant step forward.

My brain and body freeze, and I gape at the man I was intimate with only yesterday, trying to process what that action *means*. Because, because…what?

I search Rick's eyes. This can't be right. But what I see there is resignation. And guilt.

No.

Shame and anger scour my chest, leaving me hollow and abraded. As if it had scooped out everything, and all I can do is shake from the lack of whatever it was that had been holding me together.

I raise my chin, plant a shaking hand on my hip, and say, "Hello, *Rick*."

5

PEPPER

THE NAME SITS like a weight in the muggy air of the soccer field. An accusing weight. A shame-filled weight. Mocking me.

God. I'm such an *idiot*.

The other guys turn, slow as molasses, and stare with varying degrees of confusion at Rick. Or should I say, Luke.

"The Haashole," I whisper, the words barely pushing past my constricted chest. But it must have been loud enough, because his eyes go wide for a split second and then dim into resignation.

The others are here. Witnesses. But it's as if they don't exist, and the world has narrowed to *Luke* and me and the space between us. And the shame, shame, *shame* I feel right now.

He slowly tugs the questionnaire from my stiff, numb fingers, and the rest of the world snaps back into my notice. Voices start talking all at once.

"That's me," he mumbles.

I want to curl up and die. I want to yell. I want to cry. My throat constricts, and everything goes all blurry, but I pull in a lungful of air. I *will* be professional here.

Luke

Mark crosses his arms. "I don't know what the fuck's going on between you and Dr. Rodgers, or why she called you 'Rick,' but you've gotta fix this, man. She's not rubber-stamping this like Conor thought."

We're still on the practice field, but Mark's words are like so much blah-blah-blah, because me? I'm still reeling. *She's* here. The drills had been my sole focus, so I didn't notice her on the sideline until our captain, Conor, was walking me toward her.

Shit.

This is *not* how I wanted to come clean. And on top of that, it looks bad to the team. Real bad. I need to get this situation under control before things get more fucked.

Also? The hurt in her eyes before she slammed down her defenses gutted me. Still does.

After our disastrous *reunion,* Pepper took that lifted chin of hers and called the rest of the names down the list. She then arrayed us into a line and began a series of tests. We have to fill out a questionnaire, for Christ's sake. And apparently this is just the beginning. She plans to *observe* us over a period of days. Great.

Not that I expected a different outcome with my original plan other than a piss-off from her, but a tiny sliver of my ego had hoped I'd salvage *something* out of my screw-up. Now?

Shot to fucking hell.

Plus, this has the potential to explode in all our faces.

Conor joins the conversation without saying a word. Typical.

Mark waves the remains of his Caveman Bar. "It's obvious she's being a hard-ass because of you." He grips my shoulder, and I resist shrugging it off. "Fix it. Before she gets us on some technicality."

God, would she do that?

To get back at me, she might.

Shit.

"Sweet-talk her," Conor mutters, and I look at him in shock.

I shake my head. There's no way she'll let me near her now.

But Conor's having none of it. "Do it. Or we risk losing our sponsorship."

A sponsorship that had been *my* idea. I open my mouth to tell the taciturn Irishman to shove it, but it's not Conor's fault. I *did* fuck this up. And somehow I gotta fix it.

PEPPER SHOVES THE last questionnaire in her clipboard case and bolts for the parking lot. Conor, Mark, and the others fix me with a glare.

Right then. I flip them off, grab my gear, and race after her. By the time I clear the break in the trees, she's already getting in her car—the Volvo by mine, of course—and I hustle. She starts to pull away, and I slap my hand on her hood, the blue metal sun-warm against my palm despite being in the shade.

She glares at me through the windshield, eyes shooting die-now sparks, her luscious mouth in a firm line, and gives a visible sigh. She grips the top of her steering wheel, rolls her fists forward and back, and drops her forehead to her knuckles. And it kills me. I did this to her.

Chancing it, I circle around the front to the passenger door and jerk up on the handle. Locked. Then the decisive *thunk* as she unlocks the door. My insides are a tangled mess of relief and oh-shit, and that throws me for another what-the-hell loop. I don't get discombobulated easily. If I did, I wouldn't have made it through BUD/S training, much less five deployments in hot spots around the world, which were always more grueling than anything we experienced during BUD/S.

Pepper gets under my skin.

And I don't like it.

And I do, because she *can* get under it, unlike everything else.

Then thoughts of her getting under me in other ways flit through my sorry-ass brain. Fuck. See? A what-the-hell loop right there.

I slip inside the Volvo and angle to face her, the heat of her seat scorching my thighs. Her head is still on her hands, but at least her face is looking my way. Her neck moves with a swallow.

Okay, now's the time for words. Words should be coming out of my mouth. Any time now.

The A/C blasts frigid air, struggling to cut through the heavy, humid heat that's gathered in her car during practice. Its soft hum fills the empty space.

I've rappelled down ropes suspended from helicopters into hostile compounds, and this situation has me floundering? Yeah, cuz back then I had proper intel. I knew what the fuck was expected of me and knew the team and I could deliver.

This? No fucking clue.

"You're supposed to apologize, Haasshole," she whispers.

And inexplicably her mindreading makes me laugh, which isn't helping the situation at all, I know, and her narrowed eyes confirm this.

Okay, mission parameters laid out.

I clear my throat. "Pepper. I...I actually am sorry. I don't expect you to forgive me..."

I run out of steam.

"Did you have a good laugh?"

I frown. What the hell?

She straightens and locks her arms tight around herself. "Did you go home afterward and laugh about how you'd totally pulled one over on me and got to...got to..." Her brave words falter there, but horror has now clawed into my chest, and I can't quite pull in enough air.

"You think I did this to hurt you? Laugh at your expense?"

She stares at me for a long time, and her eyes register the moment when she realizes that had not been my aim. "Then why?" she asks in a thready voice.

How can I explain any of it? *I wanted a chance to be someone else with you* won't play well, and how pathetic is that? I peer out the windshield as if it'll hand me the answer and mutter, "I don't know."

By now, the last of the team members are driving out. Aiden waves an over-cheery goodbye. Fucker.

"Not good enough," she grits out. "Why did you agree that you were Rick?"

I open my mouth to tell her that technically I didn't, but close it.

I face her, gut roiling. "Pepper. I truly am sorry. I should've told you. I know you won't believe me, but I planned on finding you somehow in order to apologize. Just know that I didn't do it to make a fool of you."

She keeps that stare trained on me, waiting. Waiting for more.

Fuck. And the killer? She's got every right to be pissed. I'm pissed at myself too.

"I... Things got carried away." I run a shaky hand through my hair and then tug enough to sting. "First, it was just a coffee date, and then..." My hand drops limply to my side.

"So it's my fault? You couldn't help yourself?"

"No!" I glance out the windshield and tighten my fists. I still haven't succeeded in getting a full lungful of air. I breathe deliberately in and out. "The truth is..." I glance back at her and drink in the slope of her jaw, the line of her nose. And the steely hurt fierceness of her gaze, the now taut line of her normally pillowy-soft lips.

Since this mistake—*my* mistake—has detonated in our lives, it's only right to own up to the fuse that lit it. "I was drawn to you. A lot. And I found it...extremely difficult to give that up. Other than my lie of omission, everything else between us was real."

She scoffs.

That small sound cuts. I can't have her doubting. Doubting herself. Protectiveness surges in me, the same urge I felt when we shook hands at the café. She's special. She can't ever doubt that. Even back in high school, I saw it. An inner glow that contained a vulnerable—and, to me, volatile—mix of strength and passion and eagerness to make her mark on the world.

I reach across the cramped space and grip her shoulder. Immediately, the tension ratchets up, bouncing around in the close confines of her car. "You feel it, don't you?" I brush my thumb up the column of her gorgeous neck, her prim bun bumping against my knuckles. Her breath hitches. She has her arms wrapped tight around herself, though.

"This." I stroke again, my thumb whispering across her so-soft skin. My attention is riveted to its path and the flush marching up her neck and her pulse visibly fluttering. There's no mistaking those signs. Whatever else is going on between us, it's fucking clear that we still have chemistry.

"You want to know why?" I continue, my voice gruff. "This is why, Pepper."

PEPPER

THE ROUGH PAD of Luke's thumb glides along my skin again. I start to shake, and it's not from the A/C—it's taking *everything* in me not to unravel my arms and launch into the fucker's lap, the attraction is *that* strong.

But I'm still *pissed*, so there's no friggin' way I'm doing something so pathetic. Plus, I want to boot his ass right out of my car.

I wish Volvos came with Haashole Ejectors.

At least the anger has eclipsed my earlier feelings of betrayal and shame. But then I'm even more pissed, because anger is not healthy. Back at practice, it took all of my energy and control to hold it together. If I wasn't shaking, I was swallowing down the urge to curl up and cry. Trying to conduct myself professionally while tears kept wanting to burst out of me? Not fun.

"So you admit you made a mistake?" I clench my jaw and am quite proud that I kept my voice calm. Especially because I'm also burning with the urge to shake him and go, 'you know how wrong this is, what you did?' I want to hear him *own* it.

He curls his fingers into a fist against my neck. "Yes. I mean, no." His eyes narrow. He sighs and leans back against the seat, his head thumping against the head rest.

I hate that I'm admiring the sharp angles of his jaw and how the position defines the masculine lines of his neck instead of following through on that urge to wrap my hands around said neck and shake him. What does he mean, no?

He closes his eyes. "What I mean is, yes, I'm sorry I didn't tell you who I was—that was wrong—but there's no way I'm calling what happened between us a mistake. It was wrong of me, but I can't regret it."

Ha. I guess the belief that all guys want is sex isn't as pat as I thought. I'm so naive. "As long as you get your sex in, right?"

He launches forward, and I arch back against the door. He's so large, he takes up all of my vision as he stares hard into my eyes.

He motions toward me. "Whatever's going on in there, stop it. It wasn't *just sex*. It was—" He stops himself on a curse.

Clearly, he'd said more than he intended, so that means… That means the sex *meant* something to him.

Against my better judgment, I soften a little. Especially when I remember that I'd been the one to say it was only a one-time thing. And hadn't I used him too? To prove I wasn't the cold fish Phil accused me of being—to practice becoming a new me?

He must sense my softening because he murmurs, "Pepper," in a sexy rumble and strokes my cheek, his gaze darkening and latching onto my lips.

But the fact that this is Luke Haas hasn't meshed yet with the man I was with yesterday. Sorting out that mess is too much for me to take on right now.

I drag in a deep breath, which weakens my resolve as his intoxicating scent is pulled into me like a fresh dose of fuck-me, but I shore up my defense, turn away, and say, with as much calm as I can muster, "I think it's best if we don't…don't do this."

From the corner of my eye, I can see his hand clench into a fist. Without a word, he exits.

And in the stillness in the wake of his absence, I'm struck by how *turbulent* the air had been when he was here.

I'm not sure how to take that.

I don't like turbulence in my life.

It makes me lose focus, lose my compass. I need *balance* in my life to see my clear path.

And this guy?

He has the potential to just *flip* that table of my balanced life and leave me scrambling. Lost.

6

TONIGHT AT THE CrossFit box, it's a fucking blessing when Filthy 50 appears on the Workout of the Day board. The most brutal of the workouts, we're supposed to do fifty reps of box jumps, jumping pullups, kettlebell swings, walking lunge steps, knees to elbows, push press, back extensions, wallballs, double-unders, and burpees. All as fast as we can. And don't let the cute name *burpee* mislead you. I'm on my forty-fifth, and even I'm feeling the strain in my muscles as I drop to the floor for a push-up and then spring up high.

But each of these is properly punishing me for yesterday's actions.

I deserve this punishment.

Unbidden, a flash of a black belt lashes through my thoughts, the glint of the silver buckle arcing through the air before it made brutal contact with my skinny-kid ass.

I falter on my forty-ninth burpee, dropping my potential time by a second. I curse. It's been a long time since my old man has invaded my mind. Then again, it's been a long time since I've fucked up.

I push harder on the last burpee and make up for the squandered second. I glance at the large digital clock on the wall and note my time. My best time yet for a Filthy 50.

Yay, me.

The drone of the big box fans at one end and the pulsing beat of the techno music pump though me. I brace myself on my knees and catch my breath, my palms slick against my skin. A good number of the others in the box tonight are still pushing through the workout, and they're struggling as they near their final sets. One other finishes, and he drops onto the floor like a mosquito colliding with a zapper.

I allow myself only another thirty seconds and then jog to the back door for the five laps to the corner of Fourth Street and back. Night has fallen since I first came inside, and my existence narrows to running from one pool of light to the next on North Lemon, as if I'm connecting dots over and over.

Sarasota is a strange city. I could run a few more blocks in the other direction and be in a down-and-out area or keep heading south and be in the ritzy downtown where new money meets over-the-top architecture, dotted here and there with hardened up kernels of humanity who drifted their way down to warmer weather and gave up. One such unfortunate is in front of me, beat-up backpack on his back, hunched over and just…standing there, arms and head hanging down. Young kid too.

But this dichotomy is what keeps me in this city. It reminds me that all of us are just one bad decision away from being on the streets. And I can't ever forget that.

As my trainers beat against the sidewalk, my mind clears a fraction. Pushing myself to the physical limit has always done this for me. Helps me get my head screwed on right, as if the ache and strain is a physical thing that pushes out all other thoughts and worries.

And one thing is obvious.

Pepper makes me feel more alive than I've ever felt. Always has. I've never admitted it to anyone, but I only *feel* when I'm in combat. It's why I seek the aggressiveness of hurling. It's why I joined the Navy at eighteen and immediately pushed to become a SEAL.

Outside of that?

It's just kind of…flat.

That makes me fucked in the head, I know. And it pisses me off when everyone assumes it's a result of my deployments.

No, I've been this way ever since I can remember.

So you can see why being around Pepper has become my new fucking mission.

You can also see why I've never had a serious relationship before—not only was I too focused on my SEAL career, but why would anyone want to be with someone who can't *feel*.

Another realization hits me, hot and bright, and it's the difference between knowing and understanding. I know my old man was right about not having the luxury to make errors, but I think I finally understand it in a new way. I'd ignored my rational mind and didn't keep my margin for error minimal at the café. That lapse allowed the situation to spiral further, one mistake begetting another with Pepper.

I don't fool myself that I have a chance with her. I've messed up too much—back in high school and again now. Though the high school incident wasn't actually my doing. The ship's sailed on explaining that one.

But she has to evaluate our team for the Langfield Corporation, and I'm now her self-appointed liaison to the team.

Hooyah.

I'm past the halfway point of my run when the sky opens up. In seconds, my T-shirt and shorts plaster to my skin. But I keep going. It's not lightning.

PEPPER

ONLY ONE CURE exists for the emotional rollercoaster I just experienced—calling a friend. The conflicted feelings storming through me are threatening to become their own weather system over Sarasota if I don't gain some control. I learned early, though, that emotions should *not* be indulged. Too risky. First in high school with the shit my parents put me through, and then during my residency.

Don't get me wrong—I don't have a horrific childhood past to share. I grew up with privilege others envy—safe home, safe neighborhood, with all the comforts a kid could want. Except love and approval. I know, I know. Waa-waa, woe is me. Believe me, I know *now* how lucky I was and cannot complain, but as a kid, all you know is you work your heart out—twist that thing up—trying to get any scrap of affection from the two people who should give it no matter what. It messed with my head and impaired my judgment in high school. Which seemed to become a theme for me. So I'm starting fresh here with a clear head, if I can help it.

If I can't find a balance, I'll be at risk of compromising my integrity. I just know it. I've been hired to evaluate Luke and his team, and I *will* do my best.

Tricia agreed to meet at the Purple Chow on Lower Main—hip for good vibes, but quiet and private enough to actually have a conversation. If things get blubbery, her condo is nearby.

I spot her behind the metal pelican sculpture and wave. I haven't seen her since moving down from Gainesville a week ago, but we've chatted on the phone. First, it was all the unpacking and shopping for apartment stuff and then all the paperwork and errands I needed to do for my new job. Guilt twinges that I'm here to dump, but I don't do this often so she'll cut me some slack.

She jumps up and gives me a tight hug, still dressed in her lawyerly work clothes. She hasn't changed much from high school except to become a more confident version of herself. We've kept in touch via Facebook and my infrequent visits home, but our gruesome schedules hadn't permitted much more than that. Now that I'm out of med school and fellowship training, I'll have more flexibility.

"Still like appletinis?" she asks. At my nod, she grins.

"Good, because I ordered you one. Sounded like you needed to get right to it."

Sure enough, there's an apple green martini across from her. She takes a sip from her own glass, which has three olives poking off the side.

"Dirty martini?"

"As always!"

A bit of light peeks through that inner storm cloud as we slip easily back into the groove of our friendship. It's always this way, no matter how long it's been between visits. A memory blooms—of my first visit to Tricia's house. How warm and relaxed and welcoming I found it. How the empty glass I set down *wasn't* immediately whisked away by her mom. I'd never been allowed to do slumber parties as a kid, but since I was finally a teen, I'd excitedly packed my overnight bag. We stayed up late sipping one hot chocolate after another *without* being told it would make us fat, talking about our favorite movies and crap at school. Typical teen angst stuff.

It wasn't until her mom dropped me off the next morning and I walked along our curving walkway through the perfect landscaping that was our front lawn in Bird Key that I noticed something inside me for the first time—a low buzz of anxiety. I'd never noticed it before because it was my normal state at home and at school as I strove so hard to please and impress my parents. I hadn't felt that pressure at Tricia's, and that had been a revelation.

"How's Susan?" I take a healthy swallow of my appletini. Mmmm.

At the mention of her partner, Tricia's face softens. She's been in a committed relationship with her girlfriend since college, and I'm thinking if a relationship can survive law school, it's solid. "The arts community is good for her. She loves it here, thank God. She's having her first one-person show next month. You'll have to come."

I smile. "Of course. That's fantastic."

"So." Tricia waves a speared olive at me. "Catch me up

here. You were supposed to meet Rick at the coffee shop, but you ended up with someone else?"

Mortification washes through me all over again, and I squirm in my seat. "First, can you apologize to Rick for me? I honestly didn't see him."

She huffs a breathy laugh. "Because he wasn't there. I had words with him. He had a last-minute deposition and didn't think to text me so I could alert you. Now I'm *glad* you didn't meet up with him. So spill."

So I do. One martini later, I'm more relaxed, but I'm still dealing with that whole storm of emotions brewing inside me that I can't seem to dissipate.

She munches another olive and signals for round two. "You and Phil ended things, what, six months ago, right?"

"Four."

She flicks her hand. "Immaterial. The point is, you weren't this thrown by that breakup."

"Tricia. I named a cockroach after him."

She chokes on her olive. After she regains her breath, she says, "Whaaat? You've got roaches at your new place? They have this invention called bug spray."

I laugh. "No. The Bronx Zoo was doing some kind of fundraiser—name one of their Madagascar hissing cock-roaches after your ex for ten dollars. So I did."

The waiter arrives with our fresh round. Tricia grabs hers. "You didn't."

I grin. "I did. Felt good."

I take a slow sip, marshaling my thoughts as fresh hurt at being called cold threatens to add to my mental stew. I'd heard similar terms growing up—"aloof," "stuck up"—but I thought Phil had seen past that. I'd been wrong. I relive that betrayal. "Yeah, you're right. After I got over my anger, there wasn't much else left. Dating him was a huge mistake."

And I'm still paying the price—I'm under probation because of my poor judgment concerning him, and my new supervisor at the practice looks like he's going to use it as a cudgel to keep me in line.

"I don't know about that. Brought you here, didn't it?"

I jolt in my seat. Had it? "I didn't move here to run away from Phil."

She cocks her head. "Why did you then? I don't remember you being all that fond of our hometown."

"To start fresh," I assert. It definitely wasn't to reconnect with my parents. *That's* a fruitless cause. They're in their own bubble and always have been. The only difference is I no longer even try to gain their approval and thereby acceptance into that bubble with them. Right now, they're on a two-month vacation in Italy, staying in some villa.

Her eyes narrow. "Because…"

I look away and watch the brightly dressed people strolling by outside. "Because…" Self-reflection is not a default setting for me, but Tricia's giving me her patented glare. No trouble seeing why she does so well as a prosecutor. "Gainesville just seemed…*messy* for me." I sigh. "Okay, maybe because of Phil, but it's wrapped up in all that went into getting through my schooling. I was basically unfinished there. Working toward what I wanted. So…maybe I figured I'd come here and be the finished me." That sounded lame, but it's hard to pick up the threads of my logic and straighten them out.

She puts up both her hands. "Hey, I'm not saying the move was a bad thing. So dating Phil was a mistake. But maybe good things come out of mistakes."

I frown, doubtful. "Not sure what good will come from yesterday's epic mistake."

She twists her mouth to the side. "So…Luke Haas, huh? I don't know that I remember him all that well." Not surprising—Sarasota High had over 2,500 students.

"He's the one who competed with me every year at the science fair. Diet Coke on my winning project guy?"

She pauses, her drink halfway to her mouth. "Oh shit, really? Him?"

I nod.

She snorts, and I try to channel her patented glare. She

puts a napkin over her mouth. To hide her grin, I'm sure.

"Sorry. It *is* kinda funny. I might have had a class with him, but I don't remember. How did you not recognize him?"

I fall back against my seat. "Luke, to me, is a short, pimply, skinny kid. Quiet. And kind of a jerk. I only saw him once a year for that fair. We never shared a homeroom or classes."

"And...?"

"The *man* I met yesterday was this six-foot-two Greek god with a dry sense of humor who just oozed sex appeal."

"Oozed, huh? They make ointments for that."

I throw a napkin at her. "I'm being serious. Right when I walked in the door and spotted him, his presence pushed and pulled against me. You know? We just...clicked."

She smirks. "Is that what you heteros are calling it these days?"

"Tricia," I mock-plead. "Are you going to help me or tease me?" I laugh, already feeling better.

She leans back against her seat. "Sorry, I missed you. You're such an easy mark."

The waiter comes with our bill, and Tricia whips out her card. "Let me treat. To celebrate you moving back."

I put up a token protest but acquiesce because I'm still looking at a mountain of debt. She knows it, and I appreciate that she lets me save face with her excuse. "Thank you."

"No sweat. And I'm holding you to your promise to come to Susan's one-person show."

"Wouldn't miss it." I tap the Lyft icon on my phone.

We stand and work our way through the crowded restaurant. "What are you going to do about Luke?"

I sling my purse strap over my head. "Nothing."

"Nothing? I thought he was a 'Greek god.'"

I lift my chin and adjust my purse strap. "Doesn't matter. He's dishonest. I've also already been-there-done-that with the whole dating a client athlete. It's too complicated." Including my feelings. "I don't need complicated right now."

Having talked it all out with Tricia, it's clear that the whole fiasco just reminded me why I don't like messy, emotional crap. Too easy to lose one's way.

"If you say so."

"I do," I say way too cheerfully, fueled by martini courage and resolve. But I worry that courage and resolve will crumble the next time I'm in Luke's personal space.

The man affects me.

I can't help it.

But I *can* resist.

Maybe.

The Lyft driver pulls up, and as I'm about to step in, Tricia grabs my forearm. "Luke might not be the right person for you, but don't close yourself off to everyone. When you find the right person, they'll be worth the complication."

I give her a side-eye, but she persists. "Promise me?"

Reluctantly I agree, since I don't need to be taking up the Lyft driver's time arguing with Tricia. She was always good with timing ambushes like that.

7

I STRIDE INTO The Alligator's Butt on South Lemon Ave. My shower-wet hair has dampened the collar of my T-shirt, but I had no time to waste after finishing my workout. I'd called a meeting of the team to discuss strategy, and they should all be here by now. Aiden would've already been here, since it's his bar.

The sticky floor clings to my shoes, and the peanut shells crunch underfoot. I note who's new and who's not as a jangly tune blares from the overhead speakers. I push through the beaded curtain of a side room. We call it the War Room.

Aiden is leaning against the far wall supervising his waitstaff passing out waters. During the season, we're on an alcohol break. He nods as I take a seat. A water appears in front of me. They're so good to me.

Almost everyone is assembled. "Where's Mark?" I ask, relaxing into my seat.

"On his way." Conor takes a sip from his water and leans back on his chair legs.

On cue, Mark pushes through the curtain. "Hey, guys. What'd I miss?"

"Nothing yet, cheese ball." Aiden pushes away from the wall.

Conor turns to me. "Wanna share why Dr. Rodgers is upset with you?"

"No." While I was prepared for her to be brought up, I was not prepared for the rush of longing and regret that hearing her name induces.

Conor glares.

I shake my head, smiling. "Not gonna work, asshole. You do *not* compare to my instructors during Hell Week, so give it up. It's none of your business."

"Except it's affecting ours." Paolo clicks and unclicks a ballpoint pen. He's our Radar O'Reilly—part nerd, part nice guy, with the round head and round glasses to finish it off. He hates it when we call him Radar.

"Radar," I grunt. "The circumstances that caused it are private, okay? Yeah, I did something to piss her off. I've apologized. I think she's accepted it." The look of betrayal and hurt and how she'd huddled in on herself in the car fills my mind.

"You *think*?" Conor bites out.

Aiden swings a leg over his chair and sits. I hate when he does that. Ever since he saw some compilation of Commander Riker on *Star Trek: The Next Generation* doing that over and over, he's made it his signature move. He leans into the table, taking us all in with a big grin. "Drink up everyone! You'd think a round of free drinks would play better with this crowd. Look, I know we're all tense. Soldier here knows he's fucked up, and he plans to make it right. He called the meeting, didn't he? Let's cut him some slack."

"Sailor," I mutter, but the distinction never seems to register with them, so I've ceased making a big stink about it. Besides, the razzing is nothing compared to the shit my fellow SEALs gave each other. Like then, we might find someone annoying—hell, we might dislike one—but we all trusted each other. It's taken a while for *this* team to get to that point, but we have. It's one of the reasons we trained so hard—the more intense the training, the deeper the trust we forge. And trust leads to success.

Romy shifts his glass back and forth. "So what do you propose?" No surprise that he's one of the last to say a word. He's a quiet guy, a bit prickly, and none of us has a fucking clue what he does for a living.

I smile at him, taking a cue from Aiden to lighten up the mood. "It all depends, and I'm glad we have a scarf-fluffer like you to help strategize." Since none of us know his occupation, we always make ridiculous guesses just to needle him.

Romy flicks the wadded straw wrapper my way, and I dodge.

"We're going to make this right. I looked up what's technically required in a PPE—"

"A PPE?" This from Eamonn.

"A Pre-participation Physician Examination. Some of the tests are optional, and those are the ones that operate in a gray zone. Lots left up to the doctor's interpretation. I say we do the minimum required for a PPE, sign the medical release, and not get talkative about our health. We're all healthy, so we have nothing to hide. Our past files will show that, but no need to give her ammo that she can twist or misinterpret in her report."

Eamonn crosses his arms, his gaze resentful. "She wouldn't even be on our asses if you hadn't gone after a sponsorship."

I grit my teeth. No good deed goes unpunished, right? Jesus. "And we'd not be going to the playoffs without that sponsorship. You want to go, right?"

"More than anything," Eamonn says fervently. Nods all around the table too.

"Then this is the price, guys. Suck it up. We need to concentrate on being ready for our game with Galway New York. It's our last chance to play against another team before the playoffs."

New York is in a whole 'nother league literally and figuratively. The North American Gaelic Athletic Association (GAA) is composed of all the teams in the US *except* those in New York. They're considered a league all their own, and they compete along with London in the Connacht Senior

Hurling Championship in Ireland. Yep, they're that good. This team's captain grew up with Conor in Galway and is doing this as a favor. It's hard not to see it as them humoring us, though. The tone of their emails has all been infused with their belief that they're expecting to come down to the GAA sticks and hand us our asses.

Basically, it feels like a pity fuck.

Aiden slaps his hands onto the table. "Sounds like a plan to me, man. Any aches and pains are part of the sport, right?"

"What she doesn't know can't hurt us?" Paolo smiles around.

But everyone looks to Conor, cuz he's our captain, and we'll do what he says. I'm in this club for other reasons than it makes me feel alive to play—it's the closest to the band of brothers feeling I had in the service. We all respect Conor.

He takes a long pull from his water and nods.

That's it then.

"One last piece of business—I'm moving forward with the assumption we'll get the sponsorship and ordering our jerseys. We're definitely decided on the Sarasota Wolfe Tones?"

"Fuck yeah," says Aiden. "The Wolfe Tones are only just the best Irish rebel band."

Conor nods, and Aiden starts singing the lyrics to "Come Out Ye Black and Tans" in a full-throated tenor.

I know fuck-all about Irish history, but if it makes the team happy, I'm in.

LUKE

WE'RE BACK OUT on the pitch today to do some final drills and exercises before our match against Galway New York on Saturday. Conor is riding our asses hard, and while this kind of endurance drilling is *nothing* compared to what I went through during the third week of BUD/S training, known as Hell Week, the demands are testing the others. Just as then, it's as much about mental toughness and teamwork as it is strength, and I assist and prod the others where needed. I even share the mantra that helped a lot of us in BUD/S—focus on making it to the next meal.

But I'm relying on my SEAL training to keep focused for a completely different reason—Pepper is here to have us redo our health evals.

◯

Pepper

I divide the hair in my ponytail and give it a tug to tighten the elastic. Not counting the first day with the team—what I now call Luke's Day of Reckoning—this is now my second full session with these players. The first session, they'd been super-friendly. Charming even. Including Luke, damn him.

I prop my hands on my hips and squint at them as they sprawl on the various picnic tables and fill out their health evals. For a second time.

The first ones were too suspiciously perfect. It happens occasionally—more so with top-form athletes like these—but *all* of them?

Luke stood by me each time as if he were my damn personal mascot, bending over backward to facilitate my examination of the team. It was all a bit too...accommodating.

And suspicious.

And doing a number on my resolve to resist him. I'd successfully corralled my emotions and locked them away after talking with Tricia. In their place, I donned my cool professional manner. It's never failed me.

Though one of the players doesn't fit the pattern. The large blond—Eamonn—bounces his leg up and down. He glances my way but darts his gaze back down when he catches me looking. I make a note to scrutinize his eval. Especially since I don't have his medical records yet. Typically I'd already have all medical records at my electronic fingertips—all patient info, including physicals, are now required to be online in the United States. But this team has several green card players and expats from Ireland, and it's that bunch who have been slow to hand in their medical release forms. They've feigned forgetfulness, but I get the vibe they don't like the paperwork and intrusion into their privacy.

One by one, they bring me their forms when they finish. Eamonn hops up right after Conor, as if he'd been waiting for the sign for when he could be done. His report is just as sparse as the last time. All of them are.

Of course Luke is the last one. He saunters up, crowding my space. I stand my ground and give him a polite smile, but my body betrays me by leaning forward slightly and surreptitiously inhaling his scent. He hands his form over and lifts his brow, but he couldn't have possibly noticed my discreet sniff.

I don't think.

"I'll walk you back to your car." He nods toward the lot.

Oh. "You don't have to. I'm fine, thanks." I shuffle the papers as if it's super-duper important. I don't need more time in his personal space. It's eroding my resolve.

"I know I don't *have* to," he says, his voice low. "But I want to."

It's pointless to make a stink about it, as well as unprofessional, so I nod and start walking. It's also hard for me to emotionally sort out the man who revs me up more than anyone ever has, including Phil—who was *not* an inattentive lover—and the scrawny jerk I knew in high school. The jerk thing seems to carry over.

He does the dribbling thing I've seen him and the others do—bouncing the ball, the *sliotar*, on the end of their stick. "Look. I know you're still upset about what happened earlier this week, but there's one thing I should have told you, though I doubt it matters now."

I brace myself for what might be coming. Who knows with this guy, right?

"It was Tad."

I stop and stare. Because...what? "I'm not following."

He looks off toward the parking lot, and his jaw flexes. "Who poured Diet Coke on your project."

He's right. It seems like a silly thing to bring up now. High school was so long ago. Even so, a part of me feels a little vindicated that my assessment of him at the café wasn't *so* far off. "But you took the blame. Why?"

"I had my reasons."

"Care to share them?"

We resume walking, and now he's simply balancing the ball on his stick. Finally, he says, "It was the right thing to do." And the way he says that, with finality, I know I'm not getting any more out of him. Not today.

Why's he telling me this now, though? But then it hits me—he's softening me up. "You guys are stonewalling me. I can tell."

He glances over, but he doesn't seem alarmed. "Are we?"

"There's no way all of you are this fit."

He strokes a hand down his T-shirt covered abs. "Are you sure?" He lifts a brow.

I snigger despite myself, even though the rest of me has jumped to attention. "It's not going to work. All you're doing is making me suspicious. Especially since some of you keep 'forgetting' your medical releases. Now I know you're hiding something. I *will* find out."

He stops short and bats the ball into his hand and grips it. "Who?" His ridiculously handsome face is now set in a scowl.

"Conor, Eamonn, and Patrick."

"I'll talk to them. But it'll all turn out fine—there's nothing to find out, Pepper." He says this with complete sincerity, and I wonder if I judged the whole situation wrong. But even if I weren't trying to make my position at the practice permanent, I believe in being thorough, so I won't stop now.

"So you said your friend Tricia is a lawyer? The guys and I are looking for a good lawyer to go over the sponsorship contract."

"Sure, but you might know her. She went to Sarasota High too." I fill him in and pass along her contact info. "She's a prosecutor, but she can probably recommend an appropriate contract lawyer."

His faded, tomato red, topless SUV is parked next to me again, and I try not to read anything into it. It's an unusual type of car, and I was intrigued enough to Google it—it's a mouthful of a name—an International Harvester Scout. He stashes his gear in the open back, and I click the unlock button on my fob. But like some ninja, he's at my door and opening it for me. He leans onto the window frame from the outer side, and I slip into the gap, grateful to have the car door as a shield between me and this…this very inconvenient attraction still simmering between us, despite my continued annoyance with the man.

I don't know what to do with that attraction, so I choose to ignore it.

Seems safer that way.

But the devil scoots around so that he's got one hand on the window frame, one hand on the roof, caging me in. I look up into his eyes and catch them flicking down my body and back up. A low hum of heat builds in my belly.

"Pepper." He steps closer.

"Luke."

Jesus Christ, we sound like we're back in high school. Or at least my mocking lilt did. His wasn't mocking—it was sensual, licking at me with promise, and I had to defuse it like some bomb.

"Have dinner with me tonight."

He says it like a command, but I ignore his compelling tone. I open my mouth to say, "Hell no," but I pause. "Okay."

He looks surprised—almost like someone holding a prize they hadn't expected to get so easily.

But I figure this might be exactly what I need—inoculate myself to him. Familiarity breeds contempt, right? Because I feel as if I've finally understood my parents. After all, I am their biological offspring, so we must share *some* traits.

I'd resented Phil calling me cold because I'd fooled myself for so long that my no-nonsense, driven attitude was not coldness. I was *not* them. But maybe that's really who I am—or what I *need* to be to be successful. Maybe that was how my parents learned to survive in their high-powered attorney worlds. After all, they couldn't have *always* been that way—they'd named me "Pepper" of all things.

I almost choke on a sob as I finally—and fully—realize that my need to avoid the messy shoals of emotion, to not only maintain my integrity but also to be successful, will cast me as cold in everyone else's eyes. So be it.

He holds my gaze, and his hand stretches to my temple. He strokes the skin there, as if he's brushing away a bit of dirt or an errant hair. My face flushes. "That's a beauty mark."

His eyes glint with humor, but his lips don't budge. "I know." He bends down and brushes his lips there, and now a different kind of heat coils through my stomach. "I'll pick you up at seven," he whispers in my ear, and my stupid body shudders.

He turns away, and my knees buckle a smidge, but I make my spine into a rod of steel and watch him get in his car and leave.

Idiot.

He doesn't even know where I live.

8

I TOOL DOWN Highway 41 toward my apartment and glance at my watch. I know we're all fit to play, but Pepper's suspicions are starting to rub off.

And I don't like surprises. The margin for error seems to be widening.

I engage my Bluetooth handset. When the call connects to Aiden, I just say, "Call a meeting for six with Conor. War Room."

It's five o'clock now, which gives me just enough time to squeeze in some CrossFit and walk down to the Butt.

It's time to do an assessment of my own.

Exactly an hour later, I'm ducking through the beads into the War Room. The three of us sit down, and Conor nods to me to hand off control of the meeting.

I fold my hands. "Look. I'll make this quick because I know we all have full schedules." I fill them in and wrap up with, "Bottom line. We need to know if Dr. Rodgers can find anything. Conor, is there a reason you and the other Irish guys haven't signed your releases?"

Conor shakes his head. "Work's been keeping me busy. I'll get it to her ASAP. I don't know about the other two, but we need to ride their asses. We need this sponsorship."

"We also can't lose a player one month out from nationals," Aiden says.

"Thank you, Captain Obvious," I say, but Aiden just flips me off.

It had been hard enough to scrape up the requisite fifteen needed to form a team—fifteen who are into playing such an obscure sport as hurling, have the money to outfit themselves, and would make the necessary time commitment. On top of that, we required a professional attitude—no sense in wasting our time training if we weren't going to be competitive. No way could we find a skilled replacement in time and forge the hard-won trust we've gained.

Next year will be even harder. We're losing one because he's expecting a new baby, another is moving across the country for a job as soon as the season's over, and another is leaving for grad school. This doesn't even count the loss of one of our best players—an Irishman whose Visa is expiring.

No, it has to be this year.

We'd even gone as far as paying the travel, room, and board for the GAA trainer from Ireland to put the final finesse on the team. He's arriving two weeks before the playoffs.

The playoffs mean everything to this team, and because they're *my* team, it's important to me as well. When I left the SEALs, it was like being amputated—and I don't mean like having a limb cut off. No. It's like *I* was the limb being severed from the whole—the tight-knit group we'd become.

People have the wrong idea of what it means to be a SEAL. We're not lone wolves operating behind enemy lines like some Jason Bourne character. Our units are not called "teams" for shits and giggles. I only left because I'd grown complacent about my skills—which signaled to me that I was in danger of being a liability to my team members.

But leaving it? I felt like a highly skilled limb without purpose. Sure, I'm under-utilizing my expensive skill set doing the bodyguard work and playing as a defensive back in an Irish sport, but fuck it feels...good...to channel my energy into something safe and innocuous like hurling. Where the stakes are getting to playoffs instead of saving the Western way of life.

I pull out my Samsung and type out a text message to Eamonn and Patrick.

```
sign your damn release
forms
```

PEPPER

It's 6:55 P.M., and against my better judgment, I'm ready for my date with Luke, in case he magically learns where I live. I straighten some decorative boxes on the side table by the leather couch on the off-chance he not only shows up but comes inside.

Wow, I'm being ridiculous. Like he'd notice. Like it even matters.

But I'm stupidly glad that everything is unpacked and all my wall decorations are hung. I can't rest easy in a new place until I'm surrounded by my stuff again. It's a ritual each time I move. In the corner by the door are stacked the boxes I finally unearthed to bring to my new office—my first office. All gifts from my parents, family, and mentors for making it through my medical training. I know it sounds weird, but getting those set up in my office will finally make it all *real*.

My phone dings, and I dive for it. I'm filled with part dread, part hope that it's Luke telling me he's canceling. Until I remember he also doesn't have my number.

It's Tricia, whom I've told about my possible date:

```
Susan says to, and I quote,
```

Let Go

I frown. What the hell does that mean?

Let go of the old incident from high school, especially since it wasn't him? I hadn't really been holding onto it.

Let go of his deception earlier this week? That *is* another matter.

Let go and have fun?

Every passing day since our *encounter*, my anger has fizzled away more and more. For one thing, I should have recognized him, though even now I still can't really see it. Like, not even a little.

Also, I'd been the one to initiate—caught up in the maelstrom of our obvious attraction. Maybe he'd been caught up in it too, just as he'd said.

My door buzzer rings, and I jump. The clock on my oven reads 7:00. Goose bumps dance across my skin and converge in my stomach to swirl around.

Luke.

It has to be.

I stand on tiptoe and look through the peephole with that same sense of dread and hope I felt when my phone chirped.

Throwing the door wide, I take him in from head to toe. And then back up. The man is poured into a fitted, striped dress shirt tucked into black jeans with no belt. And there's no hiding every dip and curve of his biceps, his pecs. The cotton must be super-strength.

I swallow. "How did you know where I live?"

He smirks. "Sweetheart, I'm a former Navy SEAL."

What the—what? A SEAL? I don't know a lot about the military, but I do know that's elite forces stuff. I'm in awe. And a little intimidated. But since he's all casual—as if he doesn't want to make a big deal about it—I don't call attention to this huge nugget he just dropped about himself.

"You called Tricia, didn't you?"

He leans his shoulder against the door jamb, smirk still in place, not at all perturbed I'd caught on to his not-sostealthy method. "Yes."

I duck my head to hide a smile and grab my purse from the end table by the door. I'm pretty firm in my head that this is just going to be dinner between two people who happen to know each other from twelve years ago. We'll chat about school and catch up on what we've been doing since then, which...shit. If he was a SEAL, he probably can't talk about that. I run through all the emotional turmoil he recently caused, like it's a bullet list for all the reasons we can't be anything more than friends. Why it's important to get inoculated against him.

"Where we headed?"

"You'll see." He takes my hand and tucks it under his arm. Like we're in some Jane Austen flick. Who *does* that? I stumble, and he tightens his forearm against his side.

I don't think this date's going to go how I planned.

LUKE

I cross my arms. "Face it, you're doomed."

Pepper sticks her pink tongue out at me, and it's all I can do not to pull her into my arms and suck it right into my mouth. Feel its heat, taste its sweetness, and sense it light me up inside. But fuck it—I'm determined to show I can be a gentleman. Most of the time.

"Watch and learn, sailor." Warmth bursts in my chest that she'd gotten that appellation right with no correction on my part required. Earlier, she'd asked me which branch the SEALs served with. I'd braced myself for an onslaught of follow-up questions. Why I'd slipped and told her I was a SEAL, I have no clue. It's not like we go around dropping that into conversations at random.

Thankfully, that was all she asked. Now, she wiggles her

fine ass encased in white jeans, squints down the Astroturf, and putts her little blue ball along the curved path. The ball banks off a bump, rolls under the miniature bridge, disappears for a minute, then reappears down below to languidly roll across the lower green and plop into the hole.

"Ha!" She lifts her club and does a victory dance.

"Well executed. Now you just need to do it again for the last three." The only way she can beat me at this point.

We're at Smuggler's Cove, a pirate-themed mini golf place on the tacky stretch of Highway 41. We'd gone to the new Mexican grill on Orange, and one of us brought up this place as a spot where we used to go as teens. Now we're here, and I'm having way more fun than I'd ever imagined hitting a red ball around a cheesy-ass putt-putt course.

Pepper might have something to do with that. Mainly because she's so serious about it. It's cute.

It makes it hard to remember my mission tonight—to lessen her animosity toward me in case it negatively impacts the team. With the personal side benefit of being with someone who lights up all my nerve endings. Which also makes it hard to remember that I completely screwed up any chance I might've had with her.

So far we've tapped balls through the inside of a ship and other assorted hazards, including several caves which had stalactites that looked like drooping penises, according to Pepper. I manfully refrained from further commentary. All around us are palm trees wrapped in rope lights, the occasional banyan tree, pirate chests, and waterfalls.

We end up tying, and I'm totally fine with that, though maybe it would've been a good way to kill my inconvenient attraction if I'd witnessed her being a sore loser.

We turn our gear back in. "Do you want to feed the gators?" I ask. There's a water feature near the giant pirate ship filled with baby alligators.

She bites her lip. "I never did have the guts as a kid. Let's do it."

I swear to fucking God, there's not a movement or quirk

she does that doesn't act like armor-piercing missiles into the indifferent shell I've always had between me and the rest of the world.

I pay the fee for the privilege, and we walk over with our poles and dried-up pellets of gator food in a plastic baggie. She dangles a pole over, and the baby gators jump, one having better aim and reach.

"So Conor says you're getting a trainer in a week or so?"

"Actually, he's arriving a week from Saturday at Tampa airport. I'll be picking him up and getting him settled in the executive suite we're renting for him. He'll need a few days to get over jet lag."

I stretch out my pole, and some babies break off from the group vying for her spoils and snatch at mine.

"How did you convince him to come?"

I shrug. "Paid his way and put him up for free."

Her head jerks around, and she meets my gaze, eyes wide. "That must be expensive."

Here's my chance to impress on her the importance of the sponsorship. I pick my words carefully. "It is. But that's how important this is for us. The bulk of us have been training together for several years, honing our skills, forging a bond. We never had enough to make a full team until this year. This guy has coached numerous winning teams in Ireland and can give us an edge here."

Gator food all eaten, we wander back inside and decide on ice cream.

"Are you planning on having the sponsorship reimburse you?"

I nod. "And for the jerseys we ordered." I took a calculated risk there too by having Langfield's logo printed on them.

The pimply teen takes our orders, and soon we're sitting at the picnic tables. It strikes me that this might have been what we would have done if I'd been able to follow through on asking her out back in high school. There's some kind of lesson here probably, but I don't know what.

She unwraps her ice cream sandwich. "Okay. I have to

ask you something that's been bothering me a long time. You don't seem like the kind of guy who goes for the fancy coffee places."

"I'm not."

"So why were you at the Mocha Cabana?"

I look away and memorize the features of the couple now feeding the gators. "It's a test for me. A ritual." How to explain? "I go there because it's considered 'normal' by civilians, and it's my way of proving to myself that I'm normal too." God, that sounds lame. "The world's kinda neutral to me"—*except for you*—"and while I can *see* that it's colorful and tacky and loud, it's like it's still outside me, you know?"

Christ, that was even *more* pathetic.

"So you're hoping someday it will penetrate?"

My head whips back to her. She has the paper folded neatly back, exposing a third of her treat.

"Yes. Exactly." And the words lodge in my throat to tell her that there's no need for me to wait for her to somehow soak in past this weird veil between me and the world that's always been there—she's already inside.

She smiles, and a silent "I get you" seems to pass between us and link us more together.

CHAPTER 9

A KID NEARBY shrieks in excitement, and our moment of understanding passes. Pepper turns back to her ice cream sandwich.

I tense on the bench as she licks the vanilla along the edge. And she's doing it without any kind of air about her—totally innocent. She looks up, catches me staring, and her eyes widen. She pulls away, looks at her treat, then me, and her cheeks blush under the glow of the lamp tucked into the palm above us.

Then she holds my gaze, leans down, and takes a deliberate lick.

Just like that, my dick pops against my zipper.

Shit.

I clear my throat.

"So what got you into sports medicine?" Dinner was spent with us tiptoeing around the obvious attraction we feel and finding safe conversational topics. We mostly caught each other up on different people we discovered we had in common in high school.

She takes a huge bite out of the sandwich, polishes it off like a champ, wipes her fingers on the little square napkins, and folds her arms on top of the table. The harsh

69

light from above transforms when it hits her skin, and in this new position, it enticingly highlights the upper curves of her breasts.

"I used to be a cheerleader."

I cock my head, because one, I know this already and she knows I know, and two, it's a weird answer to my question.

She continues, "Some of my teammates were injured at one of our state championships, and, well, watching the doctors on staff made me want to do what they did—make my teammates better."

She traces her index finger across the tip of her thumbnail, and I know there's more. You don't get to be a SEAL without being able to read people. Should I push? Fuck it, I'm pushing.

"What's the real reason?"

She looks up sharply, her forehead wrinkling. "You don't believe me?"

I choose my words carefully. "I think that's the surface truth. Perhaps what you tell others, and what you tell yourself most of the time."

She tenses and wraps her hand around the napkin, a frown marring her forehead. She pushes her lips sideways. "You're right." She sighs. "I... They were injured because of me." She says this in a rush of guilt that sounds as if it's been filling her up, waiting to get out, all this time.

I lean forward. "How so?" I don't insult her by saying something like, "I'm sure it wasn't your fault." If Pepper says so, I choose to believe her. She hasn't struck me as someone prone to hyperbole.

Her hand is opening and closing over her napkin, and I grasp it. Not because I'm trying to take advantage and get in her pants. I mean, I do want to be inside her pants again, but that's not why I grab her hand.

She just looks so...vulnerable. As if, for a moment, she needs someone to hold her hand with no expectations.

She relaxes a fraction, which for some weird-ass reason makes a warmth fill my chest. Huh.

"It was the state championship our senior year. It was the first year our squad got that far, and we'd all been working hard with our routines. We had a killer pyramid. I had a major part in it—at least two girls depended on my strength and ability for us to pull it off flawlessly."

She looks down at our hands. Somehow my other had joined in the hand-clasping fest.

"What happened?" I whisper, squeezing her hand.

For a moment, I wonder if my voice was too low to be heard above the traffic behind her, but then she raises that defiant chin of hers.

"I kept quiet about a sore back. It was just a pain I'd gotten used to whenever I leaned back. There was no way I was going to jeopardize our chance. So I took some painkillers and went out there with the biggest, brightest smile. The show must go on, right?

"You can guess the rest, I'm sure. That backache turned out to have progressed from a stress to a break. It was the weak link in our chain, and we went tumbling down. Thank God, none of them were seriously injured. A broken wrist for Heather, and a twisted ankle for Jules."

I pitch forward, leaning across the table. "Hold up." I tug on her hand. "You *broke* your back? How could you not realize that? And how are you still walking?"

She gives a shrug. "It sounds bad, but spondylolysis is common with cheerleaders. The insidious thing about it is that the pain feels the same when it morphs from merely being stressed to having a fracture. And it wasn't my 'back' that broke, but a joint between two of my vertebrae."

"Jesus." I swear to God it felt as if my heart went into free fall for a split second.

"Anyway, I didn't lie earlier, though. I was inspired by the sports medics who came rushing up. It's just their impact on me wasn't something I realized until later. I think first I had to get over my shame and guilt."

"So you studied medicine…" I run a thumb across her skin.

"Yes, and after I got my MD and completed my residency,

I did a one-year fellowship to specialize in sports medicine. I don't think I would've stuck it out eight years post-grad if it wasn't a true calling. I really *enjoy* it."

And while I can see she still harbors some guilt for letting her team down, I totally get why. It also makes her a better doctor.

Q

PEPPER

I'M SURPRISED TO realize we're holding hands as we stroll back to his Scout in the parking lot behind Smuggler's Cove. His grip is strong and warm and way more comfortable than I'd like. This date isn't what one would normally picture as romantic—soft music, soft lighting, beautiful setting. Instead we're in a parking lot off a four-lane highway that runs through Sarasota, with old strip malls, fluorescent street lamps, no-name hotels I wouldn't let my worst enemy sleep in, and some rather unsavory characters lurking in dark recesses.

But it's been perfect.

I swallow hard, not wanting to examine exactly why that could be.

I'm not an idiot. I know it's to do with the man whose hand I'm holding, but I'm not ready to examine *why* that is.

The date took a different texture than I'd anticipated. Instead of firmly putting him in the "high school friend catching up" category and inoculating myself to him, the night went a long way to adjusting my contradicting images of High School Luke and Man Luke. I'm holding the latter's hand. The one I slept with.

The one who is a former Navy SEAL. Yeah, I've been trying to digest that tidbit the whole night.

Totally explains his body. I catch myself before I can snort out loud.

Earlier at the picnic table, I'd been afraid to poke at that memory of my failure—the emotions have been successfully locked away since high school. But I'd been amazingly okay with relating it. And that experience back then in high school had been a trial run compared to the emotions I had to learn how to wrangle during my residency.

We reach his vintage Scout. "So a SEAL, huh? What was—?"

My words are cut off because he's swung me around and pressed me against the side of his Scout and is kissing the hell out of me.

Instantly, all the tension that's been zinging between us all evening—hell, since our sexcapades—ignites in my chest and arrows down to my core. I wrap my arms around his neck and inch up on my toes, my breasts pressing deliciously against his hard chest. How could I think to ignore this? I'm burning up inside just from a kiss.

Granted, the guy knows how to kiss, but come on.

As soon as I get reacquainted with his taste, and my breaths are coming a little faster, he pulls away and smiles, his green eyes dark and mischievous and blistering in their intensity. He then pecks me on the forehead, opens the door for me, and hustles around to his side, leaping in his topless car without opening his door.

Okay, that was hot.

He grins at me as if I'd said that aloud, but I'm pretty sure I hadn't. I think. My mouth hasn't had a good track record around him in that regard.

"What was that for?"

"The kiss?" He turns his key, and the engine roars and settles into a purr.

"Yeeesss." I settle against the seat, pretty sure a dopey grin is plastered on my face.

"Your goodnight kiss."

"Not sure how many dates you've been on, sailor, but usually that's done *after* you drop a girl off and walk her to the door."

"Yeah, but that's not happening."

"It's not?" I hate that I sound whiny. What the hell, whiny-self?

"Nope." He grins. "Don't trust myself to stop with that, so…" He puts the car into drive and pulls out. "So I took it early and can just drop you off."

And the bastard does just that.

10

I'm boiling water for macaroni and cheese—the deluxe kind with the cheese already gooey, thank you very much—when my doorbell rings. I freeze with the open box poised to pour in the elbow noodles. Who the hell could that be? I've never had a Jehovah's Witness at the door, but there's a first time for everything.

I turn the heat dial to a low simmer and squint through the peephole.

And just like that, my nerves remind me *we're here and we're going to throw you off balance*—because it's Luke on the other side. I close my hand on the door knob. Can I pretend I didn't hear the bell? Then he holds up a box of... *something*. Whatever it is, it's distorted in the fish-eye lens of my peephole.

Oh, what the hell. I'm weak. For him.

And curious.

I yank open the door and smile faux-sweetly. "You rang?"

My heart's pounding, though, because I'm still dealing with how last night had *not* gone as I planned. I'd thought spending more time with him would cure me of him. Plus, the conflict of interest is still an issue, but only until I turn in my report. That *should* be done soon—the last three

75

stragglers have finally signed their releases. I now have Conor's and Patrick's medical histories, but I'm still missing Eamonn's—a delay supposedly due to the state of his records in his part of Ireland.

Part of me wonders if their delay had been on purpose, but Conor and Patrick had checked out fine. Hopefully Eamonn will too. I'd hate to think he's stonewalling me.

"I brought you something." He holds up his gift again. A box of chocolates. Not very original on his part, but it's also chocolate, so I'm not going to complain.

"Bribery won't work on me." I have to say it, even though I know that's not what he's doing here. He doesn't strike me as that kind of guy, and that's too small of a bribe anyway, despite it being chocolate.

He leans against the door jamb, and I do *not* notice what that does to his shoulder muscles beneath his gray T-shirt. He takes up the whole door, he's so large.

"Now you're just insulting my character." But he says this playfully as if he knows already I don't really believe he'd do this.

I sigh. "Come in." I step back and open the door wider.

He hands me the chocolate and breezes by me with a smirk that says he knew I'd cave. Part of me wants to renege. Lord knows, my life will be much simpler if I nip whatever potential we might have right now. Save myself the emotional turmoil. I'm at a crossroads and have complete power to make my path go in one particular direction. Without him.

But, oh, that other path beckons. Yes, it's lined with places I could trip and fall flat on my face, but it also seems to be bursting with so much more…life.

So I let him pass by, and I lean in a fraction and take a sniff. I know I'm weird, but screw it. Maybe I can get by on just little intakes of his scent, as if it's some drug that'll allow me to have an alternate, safer path with him.

I hold up the chocolate. "I know this wasn't meant as a bribe, but in all seriousness, you can't talk me out of doing my job if that's why you're here."

He halts by the couch and pivots, arms crossed. His large, warrior body dominates the space, but I've dealt with male posturing enough not to be daunted.

"I have no intention of stopping you."

"Why are you here then?" My blood races a little at that, as if I'm prodding a sleeping giant, and I'm not sure I want it awake. But I also kind of do.

He stands there, but he doesn't do or say what I expect—a flirtatious step forward, an innuendo. Instead, he looks down.

And it hits me that he's uncomfortable. Unsure. Not in control. And it throws me. Makes my heart go out to the Unsure Giant in my living room.

Perhaps just hanging with him a little won't cross a professional line. I'd been weak yesterday during our date, so maybe I can reestablish the ground rules. "I'm making mac and cheese. You want some?"

His head snaps up, and there's a quick flash of relief in his eyes before he shields it.

"Thanks. I'll pass." But he heads for the kitchen, as if he's been here a number of times and this is something we do every night. He settles down onto the stool at my breakfast bar, which totally illustrates how tall he is. I have to hike *up* onto it. "We're on a JERF restriction until Saturday."

"JERF?"

"Just Eat Real Food. Too much artificial stuff in that, but…" He groans at the sight of the box of mac and cheese open by the stove. "You got deluxe? Shit."

"Yeah, none of that powder mix for me." I pour the box of noodles into the boiling water and stir.

He pins me with a steady but searing gaze. "You're definitely testing my willpower, Pepper."

And then I don't know what to do with my hands, with my body, because I'm not sure if he's telling me something more here. Luckily the boiling pot gives me direction, so I hustle about the kitchen as if I'm channeling Gordon Ramsay and it's super important to get this dish done right. The whole restaurant's future is on the line.

Having him sit here on my stool in my apartment makes him real in a very weird way. "Do you want something to drink?" Shit. All I have to offer probably won't fit his food restriction. "Water?"

He takes a longing look at the mac and cheese box, but says, "That'd be great."

I grab a glass. For a minute the small kitchen is filled by the clunk of ice pinging the sides and then the hum of the refrigerator as the cool filtered water streaks into his glass.

Because small talk can smooth all bumps, I ask, "Are you guys ready for the game Saturday?"

He crosses his arms on the counter and leans forward, watching me bustle around the kitchen. I feel as if I'm on a stage.

"We're ready."

He says this so confidently. And maybe he's right. Maybe I've been quick to judge him. Quick to pigeonhole him into a 'type,' but he's been stubbornly showing me in small ways that there's more to him than high school jerk turned warrior turned jock.

I hand him his glass of water, and he nods his thanks. He isn't Phil, who was full of swagger. The man lived and breathed hockey, and I'd just been filling in his "off time." I think he also found it convenient to date a sports medicine doctor. Saved on co-pays. But not every athlete has to have an ulterior motive for dating me, or even flirting with me.

"Is this a qualifying game for the division playoffs?"

He takes a sip. "No. More like an exhibition game, though hardly anyone will be there to watch except for our friends and family. We don't have a lot of other hurling clubs in the Southeast, so this is one of the few times we get to actually play against another team. We flew to Atlanta earlier in the season to play their top team, and we play Tampa and Orlando, but we're all so new to it that we're evenly matched for the most part. But New York teams are top-notch. It'll help to compete against a tougher team than what we'll face in the playoffs."

"What got you playing? You're not even Irish-American, are you?"

"Aiden is." He laughs and takes a sip of water. "Aiden played at his college and wanted to keep playing, but there was no team here…"

"So he strong-armed you guys into playing?" I do another stir of the noodles and tap the wooden spoon against the side of the pot. Yeah, I'm a regular Gordon Ramsey.

"Something like that." He stares to the side. "I was just back from being discharged as a SEAL and looking for something to get involved in. Something that would keep me in shape as well. I saw a notice in the weekly paper…"

"And the rest is history." The noodles are soft enough, and I drain them and stir in the cheesy goodness. I divide out some for me into a bowl and put the rest away. When I sit down at the counter, his bulk taking up most of my vision to the side of me, he makes another teasing comment about resisting my dinner, but this time I look closer.

Yeah, he would've helped himself to the meal if it wasn't shortly before the game. Yeah, he really appreciates the goodness of deluxe mac and cheese. But it's not at all hard for him to resist it. He can just do it. No problem. Because he wills it. I admire that quality more than I'd like to admit.

What *could* happen if I give in to this attraction? Maybe it won't make me lose my way. But what if it does, and I cross that line again?

As I settle in and try not to be self-conscious as I eat, it's hard to ignore that his thigh is right next to mine. I can feel the heat from it as if it's already pressing against me.

And now it *is* pressing against me.

11

LUKE

I'M PROBABLY PUSHING it, with the thigh press and all, but I can't resist. I can resist that mac and cheese, but I can't resist Pepper apparently. And I'll take her however I can, even if it's just my thigh getting action.

God, I'm pathetic.

I don't know what I hoped to accomplish by coming over here. I have no agenda other than to see her again. Honest. I just…couldn't be at my place tonight, experiencing its monotony, when I could be here and feeling…something. I can't forget the taste and feel of her against me from our date last night. When she knew I was *Luke* and not Rick. Dropping her off and not waiting to see where the night could go was one of the hardest things I ever did. The truth is, the night had gone so well, in a way I wanted to end it before I could spoil it.

I also wonder if I'm throwing myself into this situation because part of me still holds out hope that I can put myself into the mix with her, and something positive will shake out of it. Boy that was a lot of mixed metaphors, but there it is.

Bottom line—I want to know if I could have had something with Pepper if I hadn't messed up so much with her.

She hasn't moved her leg.

Soon, she finishes her portion of mac and cheese, and I'm using that term literally. I'd watched in fascination as she carefully—with surgical precision—divided one third of the gooey noodles into a bowl and placed the rest in an airtight container for the fridge.

She sets down her spoon. "So…will you tell me what happened back in high school now?"

I clear my throat. "I told you, it was Tad."

"Yes, but why did you take the blame?"

Sitting next to her, with my thigh pressed against her and both of us pretending it's not the next step to…something… has me digging deeper. Anything to delay the moment when it becomes clear nothing else will happen with us. And I'll have to leave.

But thinking about that incident in high school is difficult because it brings up all my memories of my old man. How he'd insist I compete in that science fair every year, and how he'd beat me when I didn't win. To him, it was worse than just my failure. I'd lost to a girl—Pepper—every year.

I never resented her, though. Science wasn't my strong suit. Her projects *were* better. That last year I'd even screwed up the nerve to ask her out despite her being one of the rich girls. Our high school was so large, I only saw her once a year. This was my last chance.

"I'd stepped away and left Tad in charge of our row of tables." What I didn't say was that I'd left to use the last of my tip money from bussing tables on St. Armand's Circle to buy her a Diet Coke and a hot pretzel. She always got that combo every year. Figured it'd ease the way to asking her out. "When I came back, I…" I hesitate, but she's a grown woman. She doesn't need shielding any more. "I found your project destroyed. Tad had written in chalk all over it. I saw you coming, so I did the only thing I could think of."

She pulls in a sharp breath. "You erased the words by pouring Diet Coke over it."

I look down. "Yeah."

"What didn't you want me to see?"

I grit my teeth. God, I really don't want to say this out loud. But they weren't my words. They were Tad's. "Know your place, bitch."

She jerks in her seat. "Seriously?"

I nod.

"Jesus. I knew Tad was a budding misogynist. But...wow."

Yeah. And Tad, who knew I had a crush on her, just stood there chuckling as I took the blame and my project was thrown out by the officials. That night, the beating had been the worst.

It was also the last beating, because after that, I started to work out. Drew up a regimen and a plan, and I left him right after graduation. I never regretted taking the blame, even though it resulted in the extra brutal beating, because it had been the right thing to do.

The night's gotten way too serious, though, so I ask the one question that's been burning in me since I walked in. Because she just doesn't look the type.

I prop my elbow on the counter and lean toward her. Tension slowly takes over her as if she's poised herself to what's happening between us without moving a muscle.

"Comic book heroes, huh?" A framed poster hangs in her foyer. And it's from a comic, not a movie.

There's that chin lift. And because I can't help myself, I allow my gaze to drift over to her beauty mark and then down to her lips. A delightful shade of pink rises from the top of her blouse and up her neck. I harden a bit, remembering her flush the other day when I made her come. Four times.

"I don't remember you being into comics in high school." But my voice holds no censure, as if she hadn't established her credentials early enough to be credible. I'm genuinely curious.

"I love to read, but I had no time for it when I was getting my MD and doing my residency. It was all I could do to stay awake, memorize everything, and stay on top." She shrugs, and I hate that she's dismissing herself, as if her interests, or how she got there, aren't important.

"One day I found a comic left in a waiting room while I was doing my residency. I read it, and at first I thought it could just be a way for me to quickly ingest a story during my crazy schedule—get some reading in, you know? But then I fell in love with the form for its own sake. And, well…"—she gestures toward the poster—"who wouldn't love Rogue?"

Her hands knot tightly in her lap. Waiting for my judgment.

That fierce protectiveness rises in me and makes me want to help her shore up her own defenses, even if it shuts me out. I reach over and rub a thumb over her knuckles, willing her to relax.

"So that's who that is. I look forward to learning about her. Unfortunately, my comic education only extends as far as watching the next Marvel movie when it comes out on the big screen. Isn't she part of the X-men?"

She nods and smiles. "Speaking of…"

WE'RE NOT GOING to make it to the credits for *Deadpool*. We started out innocently enough—popping popcorn (plain for me), fussing around looking for blankets, and arranging our pillows on the couch—but there was a quality to all the innocence, as if we knew more than watching a movie could happen here and were going through all these maneuvers to bide our time and see if the other was on board before fully committing.

First, we shared a blanket, a royal blue one with some kind of stitching in the corners. Pretty, if you like that kind of thing. Then we kept inching closer until I had my arm around her shoulder and she was snugged up against my side. Then I threaded my hand through hers.

Deadpool says, "Love is a beautiful thing. When you find it, the whole world tastes like Daffodil Daydream."

We were both unmoving under the blanket, but now that stillness has more weight. Deadpool continues to seemingly talk straight to me by telling me to hold onto love and not to make mistakes.

Now each quiet pause in the movie amplifies our awareness. I can hear her heightened breathing. The anticipation tightening her muscles before the next crescendo of the music score drowns our breaths out. Not that there's a lot of quiet pauses in this movie—it's pretty kickass. Both action and dialogue, which would normally snag me, but it can't compete with Pepper. Not even when the hot chick from *Firefly* pops onto the screen.

"Hey, it's Inara."

"Who?"

"Okay. We need to rectify this lack in your life. *Firefly*?"

"Never got a chance to see it."

I make a mental note to change that.

Our conversation is like this, like we're both glad to be talking about things other than the tension building between us. "Oh damn, nice hit," or "Shit, what did he just say?" Things like that.

The tension skyrockets, though, when things get hot and heavy between Deadpool and the Inara chick. I shift under the blanket. I think her hand shifts closer.

Shit. I give in and lean down to her temple. I hold myself still, my lips just an inch away from her beauty mark. Her breath hitches. I brush my lips across that dot of temptation.

She's rock still, and I'm psyching myself up to move away, pretend for her I'd misjudged the situation, when there's movement under the blanket. Next, there's a death clutch around my neck—her hand has my T-shirt twisted into a fierce grip. Then she's yanking my head down to her, and our mouths bump into each other.

Oh yes.

I angle around and plant my elbow on the back of the couch and cradle her head with my other hand. With my fingers and my thumb resting against her cheek, I guide her in for a more controlled but no less desperate kiss, my heart pounding as if I'd just finished log PTs.

Just like the other day at my apartment, we're attacking each other with our lips, our hands. I stroke my tongue inside and groan. God, she tastes…tastes like…I don't know what, but it's Pepper, and it's intoxicating. And I want it. I want her.

But I hold back, taking my cue from her for how far she's willing to take this.

She tugs on the snap at my jeans.

Well, okay then.

I angle my hip away to give her whatever room she wants to take. And she takes. Her hot little hand makes quick work of my zipper, and then she grips my cock. Proving that for Pepper I have the control of a high school kid, I nearly come.

Jesus, this woman.

I drag her backward until I *thunk* against the cushions and she's stretched out along me, the blanket now partially entangled with our limbs. She strokes me once, twice, but that's not going to end well for either of us, so I flip our positions. I prop myself on an elbow and drag my mouth across her jaw to the soft shell of her ear. Her hands grip tight on my hips, as if that's all she can handle right now. I nibble her delicate lobe, letting a tiny breath of air tease her ear, and she gratifyingly shivers.

I brush my hand down the side of her neck and across her arm, reaching back to her hand still at my waist. Her eyes are intent on mine as I thread my fingers in hers and bring her hand to rest above her head. I lean away and take in her flushed-with-pleasure face, her eyes trained on mine, and her chest rising and falling below me.

Did I mention she wears these close-fitting blouses that just do it for me? The tailored primness showcases her fantastic tits and drives me wild. This one's a cool blue, and the way she's lying, the buttons look as if I could just *brush* them, and they'd burst open.

I return my gaze to hers and slowly lower myself down her body. She can stop me any time, my gaze lets her know.

She nods jerkily, and I press my lips to the space between her cloth-covered breasts, right on the straining top button. She closes her eyes, and her body slowly arches up.

I'll take that as a yes to continue.

I nudge the cloth of her blouse with my nose and just as I thought, a little persuasion from my teeth and the button is undone, but the mechanics aren't going to work this way. I meet resistance to my goal in the form of a bra. I release my grip on her hand and trail my thumb along the skin above her blue bra. My plan? Keep her distracted enough that she doesn't move her released hand—I don't need her hot little fingers gripping my cock and ending this way too soon. I tuck a thumb under the edge of her bra and caress her skin. God, she's so soft.

At first my plan is succeeding. I've got her bra pushed down enough that my questing finger can drag across her nipple. It hardens, and she moans. She's lost in the sensations, and I'm focused on her pleasure and on each detail of her skin. Her scent. Her sounds. But that focus has only served to rocket my need for her higher.

It's all I can do not to rock my cock against her hip.

To take this to another level. Fast.

So I picture the first day I had to swim the required time in the waters off Coronado and was so numb with cold I feared my balls would harden into icy blocks and sheer off.

But God, her sounds. Her scent.

And possibly because I had to resort to a mind trick to keep myself from just pushing her legs apart and plunging inside, she's able to move her hand.

And it's gripping my cock.

Fuck.

"Pepper," I moan.

"Luke," she says in a sing-song tease. Then her eyes darken. "Please tell me you have a condom."

12

I'M OFF HER so fast, I could've set a new record if jumping upright, shucking jeans, grabbing a condom, and rolling it on were a sport. I toss the blanket to the far end of the couch.

She strokes up my inner thigh with her foot as I edge the last of the condom down. Wham!'s "Careless Whisper" plays as the credits roll behind me, and I smile.

I stretch out over her again and raise the edge of her skirt. I trail my hand up her leg to where I long to be. Whoa—my fingers touch the bare lips of her pussy. I jerk my head up, and she nods to the side with a glint in her eye. I glance over. A dainty pool of blue fabric hangs off the edge of her coffee table—she'd shucked her panties while I'd been preoccupied with the condom.

I grin back at her. "Wicked girl."

She arches again, but there's a hint of vulnerability there, and I hate to see that. I brush my lips across hers while I stroke her—she's wet for me already, and I growl into her mouth I'm so fucking turned on. I'm also relieved as hell, because I'm not sure how much longer I can hold out before I drive my cock into the hot, tight heat of her.

She gives my bottom lip a nip, and that does it. I clamp her hands over her head with one hand and thrust into her, fast and hard. Ah God, it feels like an answer to be inside her again, but fuck if I know the question. All I know is that I'm merging with Pepper and all the feelings she evokes in me, amplifying that sensation.

If being around her is like seeing color for the first time, being inside her is like tasting, feeling, hearing, and swimming in color. Being caressed by it. Yeah, like Daffodil Daydream. And, Jesus Christ, I never want to leave.

I cradle her face and kiss her deeper and harder and find a rhythm inside her that has her squirming and panting beneath me. She's popping up her hip with each stroke of mine, and too soon my balls tighten and a heat coils in my lower back. I'm not gonna last long. Fuck.

Desperate, I change my angle so that my thrusts are grinding my pubic bone into her clit, and she whips her legs around my waist and makes these urgent, mewling sounds, vibrating against my lips. Not. Helping.

My mind's gone so primal, I can't even think straight, much less how to stop myself from exploding inside her before she comes. But the gods of horny-ass men are smiling down on me, because in the next instant, she tears her mouth from mine, bites into the muscle on my shoulder, and convulses around me, her hot pussy clamping down hard on me.

A fierce, primitive joy rushes through me, and I pound into her once, twice, and then detonate inside her with an orgasm so powerful, I thrust my head back and my mind goes blank.

When I'm aware again, I'm sprawled on top of her, my mouth somehow unerringly having found her beauty mark. We're both breathing heavily, and she has her arms and legs squeezed tight around me. My heart's pounding so hard against my chest, I'd worry if I didn't know I have an excellent heart.

But I can't smother Pepper. Even in the foggy, mushy bliss that is my mind right now, I know that's not good.

I cradle her and somehow make my muscles obey and coordinate enough for me to turn us on the couch so that she's on top of me. I love that she's still got a death grip around me, but worry seeps in when her head seems to be resolutely faced away.

I stroke the hair from her forehead. "Hey. You okay?"

She nods against my chest, but she still doesn't look at me. Worry now has a strong foothold in my gut.

She shoves upward and says, all rushed, "I gotta go."

"Sweetheart. We're at your place." I try to keep calm, but my heart rate has picked up. Fuck. Did I mess up with her again? "Do you want me to go?"

"Yes. No." Finally, she looks at me, her eyes bleak. "I don't know," she whispers.

I know she enjoyed it—her orgasm was proof. She's nervous, unsure, and I can't have that. My heart does a weird wobble.

Her arms are tense, delicate columns on either side of me. I rub my hands up the sides and cup her face, stroking her cheeks with my thumbs. "I'll go if you want. I'll also stay. I'd love to. I want to. But I also don't want you worried."

She visibly swallows. Her gaze searches mine, the struggle to voice what she wants playing out in her eyes.

Then she says it.

"Stay."

The wobble in my heart morphs into a victory dance. Hell, it might even be glowing and shit.

PEPPER

I TUCK MY blanket under my arm, grab my medical bag from the back seat, and hip-bump my car door closed. Today is the game against Galway New York, and I'm here in a dual capacity, which has me feeling a little on edge, as if I can't figure out which slot to slide into.

I'd be mad at myself for giving in the other night to this attraction we feel, but it seems futile to keep resisting. Maybe I *can* find the right balance and not sacrifice my professionalism for a relationship.

The sweltering Florida sun warms my skin as I thread through the cars in the parking lot and head for the field where Luke's team is playing. It's different from where they practice, because apparently the regulation field is almost twice the size of a soccer field. I can't help it—as soon as I clear the concession stand, my gaze darts around the field looking for his now-familiar shape.

My heart beat kicks up a notch as soon as I see him stretching his quads on the sidelines. Behind him, big sports drink coolers are lined up on a table like an army. Most of the people bunched around him are dressed to play, though a few people are already spreading blankets. Luke's team is wearing their brand-new gold and black uniforms with Sarasota Wolfe Tones and their emblem on the front and Langfield Corporation on the back. The New York team, in maroon and white, is on the other end. Just looking at them, there's no doubt they're elite players.

I pick a spot near the table and set down my bag. Luke's gaze is on me as I snap out my blanket. Call me a romantic sap, but instead of using my car blanket, I brought along the blue one we'd shared watching *Deadpool*. I hate that I'm a twenty-nine-year-old doctor, and yet I feel like a teenager with my first crush. The truth is, dating was never a high priority once I went to college. I was so focused on my grades so I could get into med school that I didn't have the time or emotional energy to spare. Which only intensified as I worked through med school and then my residency and fellowship.

My lesson started in high school after my accident. What I hadn't told Luke was that in trying to please my parents, I'd caused others harm. But there's more to it than that—it took me a while to realize that I'd been an emotional wreck as a teen. My confidence and self-esteem were non-existent.

My anxiety always in the background. They let their general disappointment in me show with their silent judgment. Especially with my "histrionics."

I'd been so mired, I made a poor decision. I wasn't honest about my injury. After that, career, and career *only*, was my sole focus, and I worked hard to never let my emotions cloud my judgment.

Dating was something that would happen later in my life, I always figured. When I had time. When I'd "made it." There were moments when I almost quit. Doing sports medicine might have started out as an atonement, but my fascination with the human body genuinely spoke to me. If it hadn't, I *would* have quit.

Phil was my first serious relationship, and it only happened because he was a patient first and I thought I was in a place in my life when I *could* date. And then I crossed the line with him by writing him a prescription for pain meds—hence my probation.

But unlike Phil—who I think deep down I always suspected was a narcissistic jerk—Luke is turning into someone I'm beginning to see has so much more. I started out believing he was a jerk, but he keeps proving otherwise.

I flush, thinking about our recent night together. I woke up in the middle of the night tucked into my bed with him curled around me. I couldn't help compare it to the time I woke up on the couch after a grueling day during my fellowship to find Phil, who was pretty much living at my place by that point, had come home from his game and was sleeping on my bed.

That morning over omelets, I asked Phil why he didn't wake me. My neck had a crick in it from sleeping at a bad angle. A stupid part of me was hurt that he didn't carry me to bed, or at least wake me up. He just gave me a look and said it wasn't his responsibility to make sure I was comfortable—it was my fault for falling asleep on the couch.

Fresh hurt washes through me. I should've broken up with him then. It's not that I feel like, because I'm a woman, a guy should have scooped me up and rescued me from a bad crick. No. But because I'm a frigging human being whom another human supposedly cared about? Hell, yes.

So, yeah. Luke carrying me to my bed? Five points to him, for damn sure.

Before I can sit down, awareness prickles my neck. I glance over my shoulder, and he's filling a cup with water from the jug closest to me. He keeps his eyes locked on mine, and heat flushes my skin. His gaze dips to the blanket I brought, and when they rise back to mine, his gaze is hooded. A shiver rocks me, knowing he's also thinking about what we did under that blanket. Or at least, what we started. I later found it draped carefully across the back of the couch.

"Dr. Rodgers, may I have a moment of your time?" His voice is professional.

"Of course."

He lifts his arm to the side, motioning for me to precede him toward the concession stand.

During the short walk, his presence behind me is like a physical pressure. I round the corner, and strong arms circle me and pull me back against a sizzling wall of strength. Immediately I'm in tune, humming against him. Luke smells wonderful, his soap-clean skin warmed by the sun. This feels so simple and so right, I'm reassessing everything I thought about relationships.

"Kiss for good luck?" he murmurs in my ear. "I had to get you to myself."

Shivers race up my spine again at his silky soft voice. I turn in his arms, and his intense, green gaze latches with mine. That gaze tells me that if we were anywhere else, something a whole hell of a lot more than a kiss would happen. My stomach clenches with desire, and I rise on my tiptoes, anticipation making my breath come out in irregular puffs.

He brushes his lips against mine, his hands framing my face, and somehow we keep it family-safe. But as he pulls away, he gives my lower lip a little nip.

My mind and body finally slot into a groove as he walks

away to take the field. I can *do* this. The heady, heady idea scares and thrills me.

Luke

GALWAY NEW YORK is good. Really good.

It pumps us all up. We're gonna need every edge we can muster, which makes me even more grateful that we ate clean for a full week leading up to this match. Playing against a top-notch team is exactly what we need—this is *real* competition. They not only have a coach, but two assistant coaches, and more than half their team is Irish.

And because I *am* a guy, it gives me an extra push having the woman I want to impress and whom I'm sleeping with watching from the sidelines. And her being a sports med doc? Even more so. She, more than most, understands the workings of the human body and how we push to utilize it to the best of our ability. I must be pushing to one hundred percent right now. Folks say shit like giving 110 percent, but that's bullshit. The trick is to train so hard you can perform at the level required to excel while at seventy percent. Better endurance that way. Today, I'm as nervous as the first day of BUD/S, knowing my performance was all that kept me there. I had no margin for error then. And I don't now. Because despite the beatings my dad gave me, he was right about one thing—trailer trash like me have no margin for error.

Everything changes in the third quarter. Normally the game is played in thirty-five minute halves, not quarters, but we made a concession to the Irish players from New York who aren't used to the heat and humidity down here. New players with fresh legs and lungs replenish their ranks. As the quarter wears on, it's becoming clear—these aren't just new players, they're the first string. We've been playing against their second string this whole time.

Mark's already sporting a broken finger, but he's still playing. However, Romy got sidelined with a pulled hamstring, so we're playing one down.

At the end of the third quarter, one of their forwards catches a wicked-fast pass. I could hear the smack from here as it hit his palm. He deftly tosses it to his hurley and starts a solo drive down the center of the field. Paolo shoulder charges him, but the forward recovers and nimbly bats it to another of their men. Mark flies off the ground—arms at full stretch—in a diving block but narrowly misses. He lands with an *oof* and bounces back to his feet. I'm soaking up all of it—the trajectories, the layout—and assimilating it with how they've played off each other in previous drives.

I know my teammates—I trust them. And that might give us an edge too, depending on the cohesiveness of their team. With trust, we can take risks. When you don't have that? You play it safe, only doing what's expected.

So I'm ready when their forward tries to get past. I twist and block him, but hear and feel a slight pop in my knee. We're all shoulders and footwork, the scent of fresh churned grass and dirt filling the air, along with the crack of our hurleys meeting, but I use my height and size and steal the *sliotar* from him. With a decisive *thwack*, I send it straight down the field out of our territory. Fuck yeah. Winning means squat if you're not competing against the best. Plus it feels good to take New York by surprise.

I'm feeling great, my muscles are warm and thrumming, and my cardio is handling the sprints on the field. I flex my knee and feel a twinge of pain, but it's not bothering me much. Nothing to take me out of the game. The whistle blows for the end of the quarter, and we jog to our side of the pitch. It's hot as Hades in the Florida sun, and we all beeline for the water jugs lined up on a table.

Our setup feels a little Bad News Bears compared to the kind of field and bleachers New York is used to, but I can't seem to care. I pull off my helmet, sip my water, and dump another cup over my head.

And because I can't help it, I make my way over to Pepper, even though I must stink with sweat.

"You guys are looking great out there." She grins at me from where she's sprawled back on that blue blanket of hers. *Our* blue blanket, a little known sappy part of me pipes.

Seeing her deliciously laid out below me has me thinking all kinds of thoughts about what we can get up to after the match. "What do you think of the game?"

"It's hard sometimes to get the hang of what's going on. Sometimes I'm expecting a hockey move, and then someone does something only allowed in rugby or volleyball. I have no clue who's winning. So you can score by putting the ball through the goal posts and also into the net?"

"Yeah. Through the posts is a point, and in the net is a goal, which is worth three points."

"Conor's scored three goals, and New York one, but I wasn't paying attention at first to the ones through the posts. Are you winning?"

"Nope. Tied, Galway 1-8 to us, with 3-2. The first number in those scores are the number of goals, the second are the points. We're only keeping up because Conor is a machine the few times we can get near the net."

Paolo whacks my shoulder. It's funny that he thinks he can budge me or take me by surprise. "Great save there, man. Sorry I let the *sliotar* through."

"We're getting a good read on their offensive weaknesses, though. Did you notice how the center forward always fakes right when someone comes up to challenge him?" We'd done this analysis at half-time, but with the new players, we need to adjust.

Eamonn, our goalie, joins us. "And the right forward is limping slightly. Left ankle, I think."

"Good to know."

The whistle blows again—Aiden's uncle is one of our refs. The others run out, but I take a sec to throw a weighted glance at Pepper, a promise of what to expect later tonight.

A slight flush stains her neck. Message received. We'll have to endure the after party at the Butt with the two teams, but after that? I grin and jog to position, the twinge in my knee minimal.

The match resumes, and our offense is doing a good job keeping the *sliotar* downfield, but they're failing to deliver. I keep my joints limber as I wait on the far field and keep an eye on the *sliotar* and the players' movements.

Suddenly, the *sliotar* explodes toward our end of the pitch, and their center deftly traps it and begins a drive toward our goal. We adjust our positions and move to intercept. A forward catches a hand pass and heads to a gap to my right. When he draws near, I plant my foot and pivot to shoulder charge him. A shooting pain spears into the side of my knee, as if someone's driven a damn spike right into the flesh and bone.

Agony explodes through me, staining my vision red, and the ground rushes to meet me. My cheek and side hit the dirt. I buckle forward and grab my knee. Fuck, fuck, fuck.

A whistle blows. I glance over, and the fuckers have scored a goal off me.

13

My heart trampolines into my throat and lodges there. Luke's on the ground, clutching his knee. I grab my bag and race onto the field. The whistle blowing for the goal seems to chase me, echoing in my ears. Shouts, footfalls, and more whistle blows become glaring, competing with my own personal feelings as they beat time inside me with each footfall. I can't mentally latch onto anything. Shit.

Concentrate. Ruthlessly, I shove my personal worry for Luke into a section of my brain and lock it down. Cool detachment settles like a soothing blanket over my mind and, one by one, the various noises snuff—a trick a fellow doctor taught me. I reach Luke's side, and the thump of my knees hitting the ground is in perfect rhythm to the medical scenarios now scrolling through my brain.

I touch Luke's shoulder, and he unclasps his hands from his knee and straightens out, resting his head on the ground. His face is impassive, but I know he's in pain. I quickly do an assessment of the area to make sure there's no break.

"Luke, can you put weight on it?"

His teammates help him to stand, and he puts pressure on the leg. His lips tighten into a thin line.

"Okay, I don't think it's broken, but you're out of the

97

game for now."

He curses, and Paolo and Conor get under each arm. "Let's get off the field, lad." The few spectators and the other players clap as Luke leaves the field.

I dash ahead to the tub of ice, grab a plastic bag, and scoop some inside. I breathe into it and suck the air back out, several times, to get it as airtight as possible. I twist it closed and flatten it. By then Luke is on my blanket, and I grab the roll of saran wrap and wrap the ice around the knee to prevent swelling.

Luke rolls his lips inward. "What do you think?"

"My guess? ACL, MCL, or a torn meniscus."

"Fuuuck." He tips his head back and looks at the clear blue sky. His helmet is off, his hair is plastered to his head with sweat, his knees are bloody like most of his teammates, but for some reason he's still sexy as hell.

"We'll get an MRI. How soon again until your division playoffs?"

"Three weeks."

"Well, if it's a torn meniscus, you might still be able to play."

"But not till then?"

I shake my head.

The rest of the team is gathered around but has given me enough room to work, which I appreciate. They look down on Luke as if they're in mourning. I'm also struck by how different they are about injuries than soccer players and the like. Conor has blood dripping down his neck, staining his new jersey. He received a wicked gash on his forehead and only let me put a Band-Aid on it halfway through the game—he called it a 'plaster.'

Mark is leaning on his hurley, his finger taped to its neighbor. There might be blood stains on his hurley. Jesus. The roughness of the game is definitely more similar to hockey or rugby.

"That's the game then, with two down," Conor says, his Irish accent thick with regret.

A tall, dark-haired woman steps forward. "I can sub."

The guys all turn to stare at her, except Luke, who's still focused on his knee.

Aiden shakes his head. "The GAA rules don't allow it—you know that."

The New York captain steps forward. I'd been introduced to him earlier to let him know we had a doctor on scene. "It's fine with our team." His Irish accent is similar to Conor's. "It's not an official game anyway, and I'm after some game time for the second string. We've come all this way. Let's finish this."

Conor frowns and steps threateningly toward him. "She could get hurt out there."

But the woman mutters under her breath and then says aloud, "I can handle myself. You know that." With that, she grabs her helmet, flips Conor a bird, and runs out to the field with full confidence the game will continue.

Conor looks to Aiden. "Can't you stop her?"

But Aiden just looks amused. "She's not *my* woman."

The tops of Conor's ears turn red. Interesting. "She's not mine either, ye git."

"Lighten up, Conor," Luke throws over his shoulder. "Claire's the best defense the women's team has."

There's a women's team?

Aiden nods. "Switch her with Paolo."

Conor curses but says, "Do it. Let's get back on the field then."

Luke

WE'RE HOLDING OUR own still against Galway, but I'm on the sideline fuming over my injury. Pepper's a soothing presence beside me on the blanket, her shoulder pressed against mine, her knees up with her arms clasped around them. Her focus is trained on the players, but there's a feeling of companionship as we sit here and watch the rest of the game unfold. It's a nice feeling, sure, but doesn't completely diffuse my mood. The Florida sun's making quick work of the ice packs, so we've repacked my knee twice already. It's quite numb at this point.

Pepper glances my way. "I couldn't tell out there, but what exactly happened?"

"Does it matter?" Okay. I'm also a bit surly. I know anything I say will be laced with the anger I'm grappling, so I'd rather keep my trap shut. We need to win this game, and I get a fucking injury? And allow a goal?

She gives me the side-eye. "Knowing how you sustained the injury could help me rule out diagnoses." She bumps her shoulder against mine. "If you were hit in the knee from the outside, it's most likely an ACL or MCL."

I like that she's not put off by my mood and gets that it's not directed at her.

"Nope. I just twisted. I think it was the same thing that happened earlier."

Her head whips around at that. "Earlier? What do you mean earlier?"

Uh-oh. "End of third quarter when I blocked their attempt at the goal. Something popped, but it didn't really hurt and wasn't affecting my ability to play."

Now her expression becomes what I can only describe as oh-shit-she's-going-to-kill-me. "You injured yourself earlier and didn't tell me?" Her voice is calm and cool, but I'm wary.

I lean away, resting back on a hand, my shoulder no longer warmed by hers. "It was no big deal. I was able to play." My own anger burbles with irritation at her. I know my limits. This was *my* call.

"No big—" She stops herself, and her lips twist into a funny shape, as if she's swallowed a bug or is about to spit.

I lean back more in case it's the latter.

She takes a deep breath and blows it out, as if she's in one of those find-your-inner-peace yoga classes. "Luke. I'm so mad at you right now, I can barely get my words out." Her voice does sound strained, stretched tight. "You always, *always,* report an injury."

I clench my jaw. "I'm a former SEAL," I bite out. "Believe me, I know what kind of abuse my body can take. The others?" I shrug. "I agree." But part of my pissiness is because I *had* misjudged my limits.

If at all possible, her voice gets even thinner. "Even you, asshole."

I rear back in shock, because it seems like an overreaction. And then I'm finally hit with the clue stick. Her injury back in high school. When she was on the cheerleading squad.

Shouts erupt from the field, jerking our attention away from each other. Players bunch around our goal, whistles blow, and a New York forward shouts, "We need a medic!"

Fuck. What now?

Pepper grabs her bag, but not before she grits out at me, her eyes flashing fire, "When this game is over, we are *so* having some words."

LUKE

I'M SWEATY AND dirty, and my ass is glued to a teal seat cushion in the waiting room at Sarasota Memorial Hospital's ER. Eamonn will be fine. He was responsive and able to walk off the field, but Pepper fears a concussion so they're running a bunch of tests. I've got my leg stretched out with a new bag of ice strapped on, and they're doing an MRI as soon as they can squeeze me in.

The rest of the team are entertaining the New York players at The Alligator's Butt. Fuckers.

The waiting room is eerily quiet for an ER. And too fake-cheery by half. There's a huge floor-to-ceiling fish tank near the check-in desk, and the teal-colored walls are peppered with round mirrors and paintings of pelicans and sand dunes and shit. Near me, but not near enough to be sure, is a plant on the cusp of can't-tell-if-it's-real-or-fake. It's too perfect and glossy, but maybe they just pay good money to a team of plant tenders.

Across from me, a girl with bangs and crooked pigtails won't stop looking at me and blowing bubbles with her gum. Each *pop* feels like some kind of judgment dropping into the otherwise silent waiting room.

Yeah, I feel like shit for reasons other than my knee.

We lost to New York because of the goal I let through, but I've got a war going on in my head. Part of me is shaking a fist and saying Pepper has no right to bust my balls like that, and the other part of me is shaking a fist and saying I should have come clean. It's a toss-up right now which fist will win. Either way, it's got me fuming and swirling with regret. So, yeah, that's why I'm sitting here completely worn out and at a loss for what to do.

And the zapper on this cockup is that I have to be fit enough to escort Slaine around for the next three days. Bodyguard duty. Shit.

At the next pop of the girl's gum bubble, I tell the fuming fist to shove it, because I know that's just my ego talking. If I'd come clean earlier, several things could have happened instead. With us still having a whole quarter left, we might have decided to not play any further and called it with a tie. Worst case scenario, I might have been able to do some strengthening exercises and still be able to train up till the division playoffs.

Guilt twists through me as the next realization finally pierces my fuddled head.

Eamonn wouldn't have been injured.

I need to apologize—again—to Pepper. She was right.

But how many times can I be wrong with her before she washes her hands of me? I'm not exactly projecting a solid front to her.

Pepper

It's all I can do to channel my anger into efficiency and productivity as I consult with the doctors in the ER and mitigate any lasting harm for Eamonn. *Calm, cool mantle. Calm, cool mantle.*

Finally, he's in a room for observation, and I pull up a chair. It's always a bit jarring to see a larger-than-life athlete laid out helpless under a hospital blanket and hooked up to monitors. He eyes me warily, and the instinct that has served me so well in the past with patients wells up inside. In the last round of questions, his answers had raised my suspicions—insomnia, bouts of depression, poor decision-making.

He's also the only one whose medical history I still haven't been able to get—apparently his family doctor in some small village in Cork, Ireland has retired, so there's been a holdup in tracking his records down.

I decide to cut straight to it. Catch him by surprise.

"This isn't your first concussion, is it?"

His blue eyes flash with guilt, but he doesn't say a word.

Anger spears through me. Concussions aren't something to mess around about. These guys think they can't be broken. But they *can*. "How many does this make?"

I say it calmly and pull out my notebook where I've been keeping notes on the team members, pen poised.

His lips roll into a thin line, and now that tiny suspicion I had earlier blooms full grown—these guys have been purposely thwarting me. I stand so abruptly, the chair falls back and thunks against the floor. I lift it with shaking hands, because—what's with all the anger? I need to get out of here and get my head screwed on straight. I mentally reach for the calm mantle, but it's out of reach. Yes. I need to be alone.

I push open the door and smack straight into the last person I want to see—Luke.

He grabs my shoulders and steadies me, his body a solid wall of strength filling my vision, and that just makes me more irritated.

"How is he?"

I can't even form words. The team's been working against me this whole time, keeping me from doing my job. At the very least, it's only Eamonn. Already my colleagues are questioning how long this is taking. And while I'd seen the job's temporary nature as a plus, in case I decided Sarasota wasn't for me, the other plus was that it *could* become permanent. And despite what's going on right now with Luke, I find I *do* want to stay.

Everything inside me is seething, because on top of all that? Luke kept an in-game injury from me. I do the only thing I can do at this point. I step back, letting his hands drop from my shoulders, fix him with a glare, and quick march down the hall. Away from him. Away from the words I know will spill from my mouth and can't be taken back.

Especially because—all those emotions? They'll get snagged into the lust I feel for him and the we-might-have-feelings-for-each-other emotions stupidly sprouting inside me. They'll get tangled up, twisted, and what comes out has the potential to be really, really ugly.

These emotions need time away from him to sort themselves out. Some might call me a coward, but there's nothing wrong with a strategic retreat.

14

IT'S MONDAY, AND Mr. Langfield has me on the phone. I tilt my head up to the ceiling and blow out a sharp breath. Everyone wants to take a pinch off me lately. Pepper won't answer my calls or texts, and I haven't yet decided whether to force the issue by going to her apartment. Which I can't do for another two days anyway—I still have the Slaine detail for two more nights. I've met arrogant VIPs before, and usually I just find it funny. But not last night. I lost my cool with him, and Dennis called earlier to chew me out about my attitude. Whatever.

I adjust my knee, propped up on the table, and shift the ice pack.

And now Mr. Langfield is blistering my ear. "I repeat. Either you cooperate with Dr. Rodgers on those PPEs, or we're pulling our sponsorship. We don't need the lawsuit if something preventable happens. There are other amateur sports teams we can sponsor. Heck, I could sponsor a Little League team. They're always needing money."

Ouch.

I put on my politest voice, because there's no way we're losing this sponsorship. Yeah, the Slaine gig is supposed to offset some of the financial outlay in case the sponsorship falls through, but I'd rather not have it come to that. "You can rest assured that Dr. Rodgers will have our full cooperation. We truly value your support and are committed to the team and our shared goals."

I rub my nose, positive it's dripping brown.

After we do the goodbyes, I end the call and fall back against my couch. We'd passed one hurdle since the game—my MRI showed a meniscus tear in what they said was "the red zone," which despite the name, is the best possible scenario for such an injury. Don't care why it's called that, but it means with some PT, I can play in time for the playoffs.

But without the money Langfield is forking over, we won't have the proper gear and travel money to get to the division playoffs, and I won't get paid back for the uniforms and the cost of the trainer. The kink in what I thought was a sure thing? Eamonn still hasn't been able to get his records sent over from Ireland, and with his concussion, Pepper's suspicious and has voiced her concerns to Mr. Langfield. If Eamonn's been delaying on purpose because he's had multiple concussions in the past, then it could be enough for her to bench him. And then we'll be short one team member one month before the division playoffs, and having the sponsorship would do us no good.

Fuck.

We have no choice, though.

I pop another Advil and send a text to Eamonn and copy Conor.

> Cooperate with Dr. R about
> any previous health issues
> or we lose sponsorship

LUKE

IT'S THE DAY of Reckoning. Or, technically, the Night of Reckoning. We're at the practice field Wednesday, and Pepper is all cool efficiency, questioning each of us privately, checking off items on her damn clipboard. I'm up soon, and for some reason, I'm nervous. I've been wanting to see her since the game and finally apologize, but not like this.

Aiden passes me on his way to her, and his dour expression is so out of place, I can't help but ask, which just earns me the finger.

That right there? Not normal. He's usually our fucking cheerleader. He's one of the most laid-back guys I've ever met.

Mark leans over. "Been that way since Saturday." His broken finger is in a splint.

"What happened Saturday? He played well against Galway."

"He hooked up with a friend of Claire's at the after party."

"And?" Aiden might be Mr. Amiability, but he's also Mr. Any Skirt Will Do.

Mark shrugs. "I know, right? Usually he's slinging it out from both pant legs. But she got to him, man. She got to him."

Doubtful. The day he gives up switching bed partners is the day I kiss my old man. But something *is* up with him.

"Luke?" Pepper's voice carries to me in an impersonal, you're-next tone.

I approach the field chairs she's set up to conduct her interviews and sprawl in a chair, like I'm all relaxed and shit.

"How's your knee?"

"It's fine," I bite out. But then I recall Mr. Langfield's phone call, and while it referred specifically to Eamonn, I know I need to cooperate, to keep with the spirit. Plus, I respect the hell out of her. "I've been icing and elevating it whenever I can, and when I'm working as a bodyguard or here supporting the team, I have a compression sleeve to keep down the swelling. The pain is minimal. I hope to start swimming tomorrow for exercise to replace CrossFit and do some strength-building exercises."

Her eyes narrow. "I'm not your team's official physician, but I'll be blunt. In the future, you should *not* keep injuries from the team."

"I—"

Her eyes flare with heat, but not the good kind of sexual heat. No, this is temper. Which is better, I guess, than the disappointment it replaced.

I snap my mouth shut.

The truth is, my head's messed up right now. Foolishly, I'd started to believe I had a chance with Pepper after all, but her disappointment, the judgment I know is there at my failure, eats at me. Brings up the few times I made mistakes with my old man before I learned to either not make them or get the shit beaten out of me.

Having grown up dirt poor, he wanted better for me. Hell, we lived in such a shitty trailer park, we envied the one known for lighting its streets up for Christmas. "This is for your own good," my father recited every time he took a belt to me. "You have no room for messing up." It wasn't until my mom died when I was eighteen that I learned *I* was his biggest mistake. The reason he'd had to marry her. And he'd seen it as the reason he'd never made a better life for himself. His one mistake which cost him dearly.

Pepper takes a deep breath. "Eamonn's concussion concerns me. Especially since this is now his *fourth*."

Motherf—

"Fourth?" Eamonn kept three concussions from us?

"Yes. Oddly, he finally fessed up after all this time."

After my text. I'm not liking the slow burn of anger and betrayal sizzling through me. We're supposed to be a team, and we're supposed to be able to *trust* each other.

That realization pulls me up short. Because I'm failing to trust Eamonn right now as a team member. "I'm sure Eamonn knows his limits and how far to push it."

But right as the words come out, I realize that *yes, I* know my limits. I trusted my SEAL team members to know theirs. But I can't just transfer that trust straight to another group.

A memory flashes of one of our deployments in the remote mountains of Afghanistan that the Taliban controlled. Dependence on the team is so ingrained as part of how we operate, that we're always covering for the team member beside us, no matter how routine. We were ingressing on a lone airfield and its hangar, that intel said was abandoned, during the black of night. It hadn't been abandoned, and I'm here because that time, like many others, another team member literally had my back.

That trust was there because we held our team members' lives in our hands. And while we're looking out for each other's safety and wellbeing here, the mindset and stakes are not the same. More importantly, *they* don't think the same.

Pepper jolts me back to the present. "Are you seriously trying to tell me how to do my job?"

Fuck.

See? That right there shows that, despite our attraction, we're doomed.

Pepper

I PUSH AWAY the take-out salad and turn to the computer at my desk in the practice group. Just like at home, I've already put my decorative stamp on the office. Except here, I have soothing photographs interspersed with framed full-color posters of the musculature system, another of the major bones, as well as casts of knees, feet, and hands.

I'm in between appointments, and I've finally gathered the last bit of detail to file my PPE to Mr. Langfield. My hunch about Eamonn was correct, and surprisingly, he opened up to me at practice.

Four concussions is one too many. Some doctors will allow as many as seven over a lifetime before they take someone off a team's roster, but with all the recent studies about the long-term effects of multiple concussions, I'm a bit of a hard ass. If I can prevent someone from becoming a vegetable, I will. And I'm not alone. Many more doctors feel like I do—our radars going off on four or five.

I didn't do the right thing once, and it nearly cost me everything. My parents, with their alternating bouts of silent judgment and passive aggressive comments, had driven me to excel ever since I could remember. Every science fair ribbon, every cheerleading trophy, every A, all of it, had been to earn their approval. I should have reported my injury before that championship, but I...I couldn't face them. My insecurity, my anxiety clouded my judgment, and others suffered.

I hadn't quite connected the dots until the stress of med school and my residency. Increasingly, I found I had to keep shutting off my emotions in order to do my job well. Until I didn't. I knew, I *knew*, my relationship with Phil wasn't good for me, but I'd tenaciously held on. My emotions had gotten all twisted with him since he'd been the first guy I'd opened up to, been seriously intimate with, and fooled myself into thinking he saw *me*, and was with me for *me*.

So when he'd been injured during practice and had asked me to write him a prescription, I'd trusted my feelings and emotions for him and did. I trusted him.

Only to find out I was one of several doctors he had doing this. I was put on probation with a severe warning from my supervising physician.

And I hate that *that* still didn't end the relationship. I planned to, but I was also so scared about getting my board certification after that fiasco that I kept putting it off.

I pull up the team's files and fill out the last of the report. My finger hesitates over the Send button. Luke won't be happy, but that doesn't matter.

I'm not too happy with him right now.

Bottom line? I need to do the right thing. But the fact

that I even contemplated otherwise tells me I still haven't found the right balance—my emotions for Luke have compromised my integrity.

I press down on the Send button and can't help but think this spells the end to whatever Luke and I might have had.

○

LUKE

IT'S NOT ONE of my best ideas. Standing out in front of Pepper's door. I've been vibrating on the edge of coming over here since the game and my injury, but the bodyguard detail kept me from following through. Now we have the report to tackle too.

She answers, the door opening only partway. "What do you want, Luke?" The porch light is behind me and casts her partly in shadow. What little I can see of her kicks my heart into overdrive.

"To talk." To kiss you. To ask you, are we still…whatever it is we were to each other?

She pulls in a deep breath. Her eyes tell me she's gonna regret what she's about to do but can't help it. She opens the door wider and steps back.

Breezing by without touching her about kills me, but keeping this visit professional is important. As much as I wish otherwise, this isn't a social call. No, it's now Mission: Report Persuasion. Eamonn was fuming at her report, saying it was his body, and was willing to sign a waiver. But Mr. Langfield was insistent—abide by her decision or no money. Which means bye-bye division playoffs. The team sent me to "get her to see reason."

I wanted to come here for me—to apologize for not telling her about my injury—but like a patsy, I've come for the team instead.

The door shuts behind me with a soft click.

"Luke. I'm tired." She crosses her arms. "I had a long day with patients, and tomorrow's a full schedule. Can we make this quick?"

Her abruptness throws me off. And suddenly I don't know what the fuck I'm doing. If the team wants her to change her mind, then Conor, our *captain*, or Eamonn, the cock-thistle who put us in this situation, can come do the dirty work.

And I get the feeling I'd punch either of them if they showed up right now to even ask it of her.

Yeah, I'm still stung by that cock-thistle's betrayal—and thank you *Deadpool* for giving me such a perfect word for him. The cock-thistle.

I can't do this. Not even for them. I turn and step to the door. I'm clasping the doorknob when she says, "I know why you're here."

I glance back over my shoulder. "Why's that?"

"Eamonn. My report." She shuffles over to her couch. When I step farther inside, she nods to the other end of the couch and settles in on one side, tucking her feet under her.

Jesus, I can't help but stare at that couch. Memories from our hot-as-sin sex there engulfs me. And lying on the armrest is the blue blanket, folded primly and reduced to nothing more than a decorative touch. Everything in me aches to be close enough to her to be under the trusting security of that blanket.

I glance up, and her face is completely impassive, as if she's not thinking about it too. And maybe she's not.

I guess I'm just a horny bastard, who stupidly believed we'd been inside each other's personal bubble.

I should apologize for fucking up at the game, but the words choke in my throat. I fall into the cushions on the opposite side of the couch and slouch into the corner, my elbow propped on the armrest with the blanket. I've fucked up with her, plain and simple. The old humiliation and shame from all of my father's beatings grip that apology tight. What's the point? I shouldn't have fucked up in the first place.

"Maybe you'll still be able to find another player to replace Eamonn."

"For hurling?" I drop my head to the back of the couch, defeat robbing my voice of any heat. "Do you know how hard it was to recruit the fifteen we have? And we don't want hobbyists. Going in, we all agreed to take this as seriously as if we were pro—our commitment to ourselves. Hurling's rules are a bit complicated."

"How much more difficult is it for a goalie though?"

I grind my teeth. "He still has to be smart and learn the rules so he can anticipate the possible moves against the goal. It's not as simple as just slotting in some goalie from another sport. Besides, we don't have time to bond this guy with the team, build trust, that kind of shit."

She sits back against the couch, closes her eyes, and says simply, "I'm sorry."

She shifts on the couch, and that small movement slightly shifts the air between us. The pull of our attraction is still there, but it's weighted down by recent events. I have no idea if I can even wade through that weight and breathe life back into that attraction. I suspect I'm not enough.

"How's your knee?"

Her voice is still in doctor mode, so I just answer with a curt, "Fine."

"I'll work with you on some physical therapy we can do."

Now I feel like even more crap. She's tired, upset with the team, and she's still reaching out.

I smile and lean back. "That'd be great. I've worked out some routines." I open up and tell her my new regimen and the benchmarks I plan to make for recovery.

She suggests some minor adjustments, and I'm feeling as if we're wading back toward each other with our talk. I adjust my knee and wince.

Of course she notices. "You're still in pain?"

"Yeah." I've come to regret turning down the pain

prescription the doctor at the ER had offered. I give her a grin. "You don't happen to know a good doc who can write me a prescription, do you?"

Instead of laughing at my lame attempt at a joke, Pepper goes rigid, and her face drains of all color.

"You're asking me to write you a prescription?"

"No. I—"

But she's launched herself off the couch and rounds on me, fists on her hips. "First, you kept Eamonn's concussions from me. I told myself you weren't being so solicitous for the sake of the team—"

At this, I lean forward. I resist standing because I don't want to accidentally use my height and strength to intimidate her. "I didn't know about Eamonn. Believe me, I'm pissed at him too."

But she keeps going. "—and now you're plying me for drugs? Is that why you really came tonight?"

What the—?

An icy deluge of reality hits me as if a bucket of cold water has been poured over my head, and it leaves me shaking. I'm *not* some stereotypical trailer park punk, but apparently she still views me that way despite everything.

"I was *joking,* Pepper," I say with as much calm as I can manage.

15

GOD, I HAVE to get him out of here. Luke's presence—taking up all the space he does with his emotions and hunkiness and all the unsolved mess wrapped up in potential—is like an unchecked item on my to-do list, and I don't want it. I don't have time for it. I don't have the energy for it. Moving here is my chance to finally be the doctor I've worked so hard to become. The other doctors in the practice took a chance on hiring me fresh from my fellowship and with a probation looming over me, and how I handle this year will determine if I've made a case for myself—to expand their practice with *me* in that slot.

And this fledgling-whatever-the-heck-it-is relationship jeopardizes that.

If he leaves, that item will no longer be on my to-do list. Simple as that.

I walk to the door. Fully aware of his stare on my back the whole time. I open the door, and a sharp intake of breath pierces the air behind me. And because I'm an adult, I turn and look him in the eye. There's hurt there. But also a sort-of resignation I don't want to examine.

For a second, he remains on the couch, his eyes boring into me, his body tensed. Stubborn. And is it my imagination

115

that his hand seems to caress the corner of the blue blanket?

My throat thickens—I'm totally being the cold bitch that Phil always accused me of being. Well, so be it. That's me. My relationship with Phil had messed with the delicate balance I'd achieved between my professional and personal life. And now with Luke? Who churns up way more emotions? No way.

A part of me knows I'm being unfair, but I have to protect *myself* first.

He uncoils to his full height, every movement measured and controlled. And he nods, his gaze never breaking from mine. Without a word, he walks by me, and I lean forward before I can catch myself and take a tiny sniff.

Dammit. I'm not the kind of woman who sniffs at guys.

The ice I siphon into me keeps me poised until he exits and the door snicks shut. Then a flash of heat and anguish rushes through me, melting that ice, that poise.

I shuffle to the kitchen and hike up onto the stool. A flower vase with fresh asters from Publix sits in front of me.

What the hell is wrong with me? Had I been expecting a protest? I twist the vase around and around in circles on its base.

No.

No. Shit. What's bothering me is that I'd felt more for him than I realized, and it guts me that it's over before it can really get going.

I shove the vase away. All these tangled up emotions that I can't sort also proves I've got no bandwidth for a relationship right now.

Luke

The CrossFit sessions have come and gone this evening, so I head to the nearby late-night gym. The pissed-off that's roiling inside me needs purging, and swimming won't cut it. Pepper's accusations and calm dismissal have me all messed up, and I need to push myself. Yeah, the PT doesn't want me running yet, but I can't seem to care. When I reach the treadmill, I tilt that sucker up and set a punishing pace.

In addition to the punishment for fucking up, maybe if I push myself to exhaustion, I can become numb again. Unfeeling.

Funny. I craved being around her because she broke through the perpetual gray that cloaks me, but now I'm *all* feeling—like a live, exposed wire—and I want that numbness back.

A gym rat climbs onto a machine next to me, sees my settings, and adjusts his to the same.

Really?

I chuff a laugh and up the ante without even glancing his way. It's not at the level I normally do, but he can't compete with even an injured me.

And sure enough, after upping his to match my low-for-me setting, a desperately disguised wheezing reaches my ear, and his face turns red. He rolls off and limps to the locker room.

Stupid fucker. Know your limits. I know mine, and I'd stupidly tried to reach for more with Pepper.

Then I curse and hit the stop button. What the fuck am I doing on a fucking treadmill? I pride myself on knowing my limits and got butthurt because she didn't trust me. But trust goes both ways. And this right here? Running on a treadmill with a torn meniscus puts the lie to my judgment.

Pepper

Tricia and I are ensconced at the bar of the Purple Chow

having a quick lunch before we both have to head back to work. Of course, she's noticed my mood. It's been two days since I've seen Luke, and frankly, I'm not sure what to make of myself or the situation.

Yes, I've looked back at our conversation and seen that I'd jumped to conclusions about his request for a scrip. I *should* have given him the benefit of the doubt. But the larger problem still remains.

"Let me get this straight. You kicked him out of your house because you didn't want to deal?"

"Er, yes…" I did the right thing. I need this job to be permanent. I can't afford to sacrifice my job for my personal life.

I'm devastated about ending things with him, though. Both nights, I cried myself to sleep and woke up with swollen, grainy eyes. But I take a shower, drink my cup of tea, and stick to my new routine. Somehow I get through the day, although at first I worried about it affecting my decision-making abilities. I've operated on less sleep, though. I guess that's what the grueling hours of med school and residency train you for.

She wipes her mouth. "And how do you feel about that decision now?"

I push the last bit of soft taco to the edge of my plate. "I'm miserable."

"So you opted to forgo working things through with him to avoid emotion, and you haven't avoided it."

I slump. "I thought I could just shove it away and get on with my career."

"What are you afraid of…really?" She puts down her fork with a clatter and faces me with her prosecutor stare. "I think you're afraid of your own feelings."

I jerk at that. "No. You don't get it. Whenever I let my feelings rule me, my career suffers."

"Is this about your cheerleading accident?"

"Not fully, but it was a symptom of the problem."

"Catch me up here."

I blow out a breath. "Whenever I get caught up in

emotions, my judgment gets impaired."

"Like not telling anyone about your injury."

"Exactly." I slump with relief at not having to explain. Tricia knows what it was like for me in high school.

"That was a long time ago, sweetie. You've matured."

I straighten. "No. It was the beginning of a pattern. There was this one time. During my fellowship…" I fill her in on the trouble I got into with writing a scrip for Phil because I'd been too wrapped up in our relationship. I should feel ashamed at not only having to share this black mark with my best friend, and what she must now think of me, but also because I *did* keep it from her, but honestly? I'm all tapped out right now. I'm kind of in fuck-it-all mode.

"So when Luke asked you for a prescription…"

"Yeah. I flipped." And since I need to be honest, I correct her. "Technically, he didn't ask. He only jokingly asked if I knew a good doctor who would write one. Trish…I just… He morphed into Phil right then, and I didn't stop to evaluate. See, my judgment gets impaired when I'm emotional."

She purses her lips. "Has your work suffered this week, though?"

I push my food around some more. "Actually, no."

"Then why do you feel like you still can't make judgment calls? You're emotional now about Luke, right?"

"I hesitated in making the right call on Eamonn because of my feelings for Luke."

"But you still ended up making the right call…"

"Yes, but I pushed Luke away without giving him a chance."

"Okay, so you have some work to do in your *personal* life, but, sweetie, I think you have your professional life down pat. Stop letting your fear of emotions dictate your life."

She's right. I've been too afraid of strong emotions my whole life, and it's time I stopped. I've always worried that they'd affect me professionally.

"I'd…I'd like to fix things with him. But I messed up his team's chances."

"I'm not sure you need to fix his team. But remember

what I said earlier. When you find the right person, they'll be worth the complication." She places cash on her bill and stands. "Speaking of complications that are worth it, Susan's so nervous about the opening, it's making *me* nervous. See you tomorrow night? I need you for moral support."

Pepper

THE REST OF the afternoon, between appointments, I think about what Tricia said.

I did screw up by throwing Luke out that night.

And I want to make it right with him. I *trust* he wouldn't ask me to be unethical. Though I won't change my report—that was the right thing to do—I *can* offset its effect. The thank you postcard from the Bronx Zoo arrived in the afternoon's mail, and it's given me an idea.

Of course I run through the pros and cons of bringing Phil back into my life, even peripherally. If it will go toward making things right with Luke? Because I also realized that, no, I do *not* want to end up like my parents—cold and... and fake. Just because that's how they ended up doesn't mean I have to.

I hover over the keyboard and type:

```
Hi Phil,

Been awhile. Listen...
```

Can I do this? Just the thought of being in the same room as him, much less talking to him, has me pulling my fingers away. Gah. I look at the wall clock and minimize the screen just as the buzzer rings for my next appointment.

I help the next patient, write a prescription, and pull up the email again. And drum my fingers over the table.

I type a few more sentences. And the anxiety of dealing with him washes through me again. I fish out the postcard and flip to the back. The words greet me again, "Meet Phil Stoddart." A giggle bursts past my lips, and I prop it up against the screen with Phil the Madagascar hissing cockroach staring back at me.

Fuck it.

What is Phil to me? Nothing. He has no power over me. If this helps Luke, then I'll do it. He and his team still want to go to the playoffs, and maybe I can help.

16

SOFT JAZZ COILS through the swanky, white-walled gallery on Upper Main and mixes with the low hum of conversation and the occasional cultured chuckle.

Susan's artwork graces the walls with track lights angled for optimum viewing. I grab white wine from the table in the corner and thread back through the patrons to where Tricia and Susan are holding court. The gallery owner is placing an orange Sold dot on a nearby painting, which happens to be my fave of hers too—a semi-abstract of two lovers entitled, "Eros and Psyche After the Trials." Susan's emitting that need-to-act-cool-but-I-really-want-to-dance-a-jig glow.

I lean over and whisper, "Congrats." I really am happy for Susan, and my own turmoil has no place here.

Susan grins, and Tricia wraps her hand in hers and gives it a squeeze, pride clear in her features and her stance.

"I think we should celebrate your opening and your sale." I lift my glass of wine.

Tricia grins. "I agree. Susan, your choice. Anything but—"

"The Alligator's Butt!"

Tricia groans, so that must have been what she'd been about to say. "Alligator's Butt it is." She looks at me and rolls her eyes. "It's a new bar on South Lemon Ave, and Susan has an unnatural love for the Butt."

Susan elbows her. "Hey, they've got great margaritas."

I laugh. "Then it has my vote. I'm always up for a new place. Let's go!" I look around. "Well, as soon as this is over, I mean."

"Shouldn't be much longer."

My phone chirps, and I look at the text. It's Phil. Normally, I'd stuff it back into my purse, but I've been waiting for this.

> Hi, babe. I'm in town now. Just checked in at a hotel on University Parkway. Can we meet tonight to discuss this?

Babe? I'll need to nip that in the bud. Suddenly, what I thought had been a great idea—invite Phil to meet the team and see if he can stand in for Eamonn—doesn't seem like such a great idea.

"Hey, guys, are you okay with my ex meeting us there?"

Tricia's gaze snaps to mine. "What are you doing?" she asks, her voice low and cautionary.

I wave her off. "*So* don't need to worry about me going there again. But I need to talk to him in public."

She narrows her eyes but gives a nod.

LUKE

WE'D BEEN NURSING beers in the War Room, but then we all got sick of our own company and our moping. The others are moping about the playoffs being unattainable. I am too, but not as much as I am about Pepper and how I blew it with her. The team and the camaraderie were the world to me. Helped me stay centered. But it hadn't been quite what I'd thought it was.

Also, now that I've been with Pepper and see how things *could* be, the team's not near enough. And—because I fucked up—that Pepper-filled future is not even remotely possible.

We'd achieved our team goal—getting the money to get us to the championship—but that no longer matters since we're short a member. Conor had Tricia's lawyer buddy read over the sponsorship contract, and then he signed it. I'm reimbursed for the jerseys. And, yeah…

We moved out into the main part of the bar to play darts. Aiden still hasn't snapped out of his glum mood from a week ago. Claire is here, as usual, but she and Conor are at opposite sides, taking great pains to ignore each other. I resist rolling my eyes. Instead, I take aim, and the dart flies true, *thunking* into the cork. Bullseye.

Out of the corner of my eye, I see three women enter the bar, and the hairs on the back of my neck rise in recognition. One of them's Pepper. And I know I have to make eye contact with her before she has a chance to see me and leave.

I drag the chalk across the board, marking my score, and stalk her way. My knee, still wrapped up tight, gives me no trouble, though it does make my gait stiff. Her head lifts at that moment, and her gaze locks with mine. A cocktail of emotions rises up within me and powers my steps. The lust and rightness that's always there, sure. Chief among them, though, is contrition.

I've gotta man up and apologize. I'd let my pride get in the way. Trust goes both ways, and I shouldn't have just assumed I had hers. I need to earn it, and I've done a piss-poor job with that.

They congregate around one of the high tables dotting the place, and when I arrive, I stick on a smile. "This round's on me. What will it be, ladies?"

"Luke?" says one of the friends with her, and I finally look at her companions.

"Tricia? Hey, sorry, it's been a long time. How are you?" We'd had a physics class together senior year, and I always thought she was a level-headed chick. We do the polite, quick catch-up one does when running across someone you don't know too well, and I'm soon back with their drinks.

Pepper hasn't said a word other than her drink order. I wish I had a chance to do this privately, but she's here now, and fuck if I let the opportunity go by. Her silence, though, is almost like a physical push against my side.

"Pepper."

"Luke?"

Her tone is cool, but there's a faint thread of playfulness, and I snatch that thread as if it leads to a life preserver. The words that need to come up through me, they're like razor blades, but I force them through. "I'm sorry."

There. That wasn't so bad. Still won't make the outcome any different, but there's a strange catharsis with the words, as if the razor blades are scraping off unneeded junk inside me and leaving me cleaner.

I edge closer. "I'm sorry I was such an ass. And that I worked against you with the team. Kept my injury from you. I also would never ask you to compromise your professional ethics. You need to know that."

I sip from my beer to clear the burn left from the words, but I don't regret saying them. Still makes me an ass for having done all that, but that's reality. Her judgment will be deserved.

Pepper nods and watches me for a short bit, her face unreadable. I resist the urge to squirm. I'm a fucking Navy SEAL, but what this woman does to me makes me act outside of the normal parameters.

She lifts her drink in a toast-gesture. "Apology accepted." She sets her drink down without taking a sip. "But I need to talk to you privately."

"Sure. I'll be at the darts board when you're done here."

I lift off the stool—I said what I came to say—when a blond jock approaches the table, his gaze fixed on Pepper.

The table immediately grows quiet, and Tricia darts a glance my way. The newcomer's a little too smug for my taste. I'm sticking around for this. I don't care if it sounds all primitive. If she asks me to leave, though, I will.

He leans down, clearly going for a kiss, but Pepper turns her head and changes it to a cheek-kiss. Still makes my blood boil.

Doesn't faze Blond Schmuck. Instead, he says smoothly, "Hey, babe."

My fists clench. Babe?

But I'm watching the non-verbal cues, and this isn't welcome on her part. Her friends also only look tolerant. Yeah, I'm sticking around for this, but not to piss a circle around her and mark her as mine, just as back-up. Three friends at the table are better than two, right? Though of course I *do* want to piss a circle around her. Some things are hard-wired in the male brain, I guess.

Pepper gives a tight smile and turns to us. She barely glances at me and says to the group, "Everyone? This is Phil. My ex-boyfriend." Is it my imagination, or does she place an extra emphasis on the *ex* purely for Phil's benefit and not mine? "Phil, this is Tricia, Susan, and Luke."

Phil puts on a huge grin and glad-hands everyone as if he's some fucking politician. I give his handshake an extra squeeze, but he doesn't flinch or retreat.

"Luke. I'm glad you're here," she says to me, and I perk up, thinking she wants me to play the Love Interest to deflect Phil's obvious interest. Their relationship might be over for her, but this guy hasn't accepted that memo.

"Phil's a goalie for a semi-pro hockey team in Gainesville. I invited him here to replace Eamonn if your team's captain will have him." She waves at me and turns to her ex. "Luke's on the team and can get you up to speed on the rules and where they practice. Introduce you."

He grins at everyone like he's just saved the day. "Great. Glad to be here. Sounds like an interesting sport."

"It is," I say cautiously. Pepper called him in to help our

team? I don't know what to make of that. "We have a practice tomorrow actually, despite not having enough to make a team. I can give you the details."

Phil curls a hand onto Pepper's shoulder, and it's all I can do not to launch across the table and knock that hand away. But Pepper's a grown woman and can take care of herself. I might have growled, though, and Tricia gives me an amused eyebrow lift. I pretend it wasn't me.

"I look forward to it. Anything to help out Pepper."

Tricia swirls her margarita glass and licks up some salt from the rim. "I thought you two called it quits."

Phil chuckles. "What does that matter? I'm here now."

Pepper shrugs his hand off her shoulder, and I do a mental fist pump. "I'm sorry, Phil. I think you've gotten the wrong impression here. My invitation had no ulterior motive."

Some of his swagger fades, but he gamely presses on. "You tell yourself that, but we both knew you'd come around."

"Come. Around?" There's a chill in her posture, but Phil is completely clueless. For the first time tonight, I'm feeling a little light. This event has popcorn potential. Heck, I'm getting popcorn. Like any good bar, Aiden has a machine for patrons, and it's right behind me.

I hotfoot it over, grab a bowl, and settle in for the show. I return in time to hear Pepper say, "You broke it off to get me to quote, 'see the light'?"

Uh-oh.

17

I TAKE A handful of popcorn and pass it to Tricia. Phil seems completely oblivious that he has an audience.

He tries the shoulder-rub move, and Pepper shrugs him off again.

"Aw, babe. We were good together. I just needed to give you time to see it."

She levels him with a get-real stare. "Phil. You called me a cold fish."

Wait. What? I glance at Pepper and then at Phil. He's even more of a bonehead than I thought. I almost feel sorry for him. Not really.

Phil digs his hands into his front pockets and rocks back on his heels. "I just needed to push you some. Get you to see what you were missing."

Pepper straightens and pulls up a bright smile. "It worked." It fools Phil, who steps closer, a corresponding grin on his smarmy face, but it doesn't fool me. I eat another handful of popcorn. Pepper's got this.

"I learned exactly what I was missing." She pauses. "Nothing."

Phil stops mid-step and rears back, a look of disgust and disbelief on his face. "God. You really *are* a cold bitch."

I must have tensed, because Tricia puts a cautioning hand on my thigh, but I brush it off. "Watch it, Phil." I put full-on testosterone into his name.

The asshole starts and glares at me and then at Tricia and Susan. His lip curls. "Whatever." He pushes away from the table. "I don't know why I bothered." He points a finger at me. "And don't fool yourself into thinking you can get in her pants by defending her. That shit don't work with her, so you're barking up the wrong tree."

What a tool. Before I can say a word, Pepper throws a napkin on the table. "I don't know why I thought this could be a solution for the team. I believed you had one mature bone in your body, Phil. Looks like I was wrong."

He whips his gaze back to her. "I don't know what your problem is. But it's no longer mine. You'll end up alone with your attitude."

I unclench my jaw and my fists and say calmly, "And what attitude is that?"

Yeah, I should back off for a number of reasons. Pissing him off won't convince him to stand in for Eamonn. And I *do* know Pepper well enough to know she doesn't need a man to fight her battles. But I can't let this stand. I've already screwed up with her anyway, so I have nothing to lose.

And the thing is—Pepper's part of my inner team even though she doesn't want to be there. Maybe this jerk could work out for the team, and we'd go to the playoffs. But not at the expense of Pepper.

Asshole crosses his arms. "Her cold bitch routine."

"Let me get this straight," I say as I kiss the playoffs goodbye. "She's a cold bitch because she knows her mind, can express it eloquently, and the end result is that she doesn't want you?"

All three women turn to stare at me. But I can't stop. "News flash, buddy. The world doesn't revolve around you. And maybe, just maybe, you only think she's cold because you didn't have the *heat* to be admitted into her circle of trust." We'd had that heat. But I'd broken her trust. And now I'm back outside. Doesn't make her cold, though.

Pepper jerks toward me at that and looks at me with surprise and then…Jesus…*heat.*

Phil looks poleaxed for a moment. Clearly, no one's ever called him on his shit, but he also notices the undercurrent between Pepper and me, and what it means. "Fuck you." He walks around the table as if he's going to have a go at me. I stand to my full height, and he stops.

"No, thanks." I cross my arms. "I don't swing that way." It's a cheap, throwaway line, but most of my mental energy is being spent in not punching this asshole in the face.

Phil pivots back to the table and sneers at Pepper. "Whatever. I'm out of here."

She serenely nods. "I'll get the team details and text them to you."

He rears back. "You must think me an idiot if you think I'll play for this team of yours." He gives me a parting look and storms off.

I watch him retreat until his ass is on the other side of the door. Then I turn back to the table. I nod to Tricia. "Let the record show, counselor, that I did *not* punch that asshole and bust his nose like he deserved."

I nod at Pepper and step away, because the last thing I want her to think is that I'd done it for show. That I'd done it to 'get in her pants' like Phil insinuated.

No. I'd done that because it burned me, searing my guts, to have someone disparage Pepper. She didn't deserve that. At all.

Playoffs be damned.

I head for the door, palming my keys. Pepper's gaze behind me feels physical—a weight at my back, urging me to turn around. But I resist.

Her attempt to help the team is…awesome, but I don't fool myself that it means more than what it is. Besides, it doesn't hold the same importance for me as it once did. My narrow-band focus on the team and their wants spoiled any chance I had with Pepper. I rub my chest where a hollowness seems to have become my new norm.

I'm halfway around the corner, when the door opens behind me. It's not her, I tell myself, though the dumb part of my body perks up with hope. But then light steps hurry toward me, and the skin on the back of my neck prickles.

"Hi, Pepper," I say softly without turning around. And without any discussion, she falls into step beside me as we stroll to the parking lot. I see the bumper of her Volvo and steer us toward it. I have no clue what to say or what to make of this. My throat is choked up with words, and none of them will probably be right. All I know is that I'm vibrating with the energy I feel whenever I'm around her. And I'll stick to her side to keep feeling this until she tells me to scram. Which will probably be soon.

At her car, I'm prepping my goodbye. She has no more reason to come to our practices. I do need to thank her for trying to get Phil here, even if he turned out to be a douche.

We both stand at her car door. Awkwardly. As if we're back in fucking high school. She twists her key fob in her fingers, and I say, "Pepper" at the same time she says, "Luke."

We both laugh, and that gives us forward momentum. She angles her head to her car. "Can we talk?" She hits the unlock button and opens her door.

My heart gives a hard kick. Hell, yes.

I fast-walk around the hood before she can change her mind and lock the doors. My mind flashes back to nearly two weeks ago when I'd messed up bad and got in this car and stumbled through an apology.

I fold myself into her passenger seat and gently shut her door. She's got her A/C on full blast, but the radio is turned down, a bare suggestion of a jangly tune coming from the speakers.

I twist my bulky body around so that I'm facing her but remain quiet. She's steering this convo, and I don't want to fuck it up by saying the wrong thing. Again.

She mirrors my position and stares at me a minute.

Fuck, it's killing me to be this close and not be able to

touch her. In the close confines of the car, her soft breathing and her scent starts to fill the space.

"I want to apologize," she says softly but with strength.

That throws me. "For what?"

"For pushing you out of my house the other night without talking things out with you. For assuming the worst of you."

While her words make sense, I'm still tense, waiting for the proverbial blow. "You were upset with me. I totally understand."

"No. You don't." She sighs and looks at a spot over my shoulder. "I was pushing you away because…because I didn't want to wade through all this to see what could be."

I cock my head. Some of my confusion must show, because she continues.

"I want to explore what we have going on between us, but…" She blows out a breath. "But you need to know why I overreacted." She fills me in on how Phil had used her as one of his sources for pain meds. Good thing that fucker is gone, because I'd like to punch him even more now.

She continues, "I'm…I'm not so good with emotions. I think I knew deep down you weren't asking me to be unethical, but it just reminded me so much of how Phil had used me. I was tired, and I panicked and kicked you out because I worried about my emotions affecting me professionally." She looks directly at me and bites her lip. "And that's not fair to you. Or me."

My stomach churns. Part of me is elated, but the other part is scared shitless. Why is she giving me another chance? I fucked up. And I'll fuck up again, I'm sure. She *knows* this.

Though it pains me, I gotta come straight. I can't get into a relationship with her if it's going to end in a flaming pile of my fuckups.

I clear my throat. "I can't be what you need."

18

SHE PULLS BACK. Then her eyes narrow. "What do you mean? What do I need?"

My fist clenches, and I rub it against my knee. "Not me, for damn sure. I rarely mess up, but I seem to be prone to it with you. You deserve better."

"I think I can judge what I need."

"See? I don't say the right thing."

She stares at me for a moment. "What does messing up mean to you? I feel like I'm missing something here."

I shift in my seat because she's hit on something I can't quite name. It's like a big ball of confusion and hurt and inadequacy, and it's been there, lodged in my chest, ever since I can remember. Most of the time I'm not conscious of it. But when I fuck up, it's there, ready to wash me in inadequacy.

She leans forward. "You apologized. I accepted your apology and forgave you. I just apologized to you. Do you forgive me?"

I frown. "Of course."

"Do you think any differently of me for having apologized?"

"Nooo…" Owning up to mistakes is the right thing to do. Only insecure cowards deflect. The trick was not making

133

them in the first place.

I don't know where she's going with this, but it's nudging at that ball, threatening to bust it open in my chest. I'm not sure I want that, but damned if I'll get out of this car right now.

She cocks her head, looking at me as a bird might look at a questionable meal. "But you're confused about why I want to pursue things with you." She reaches forward and tentatively touches my knee. I jerk at the unexpected touch, and instantly the space feels smaller between us, zinging with awareness.

"I know you feel this. So it's not that." She pins me with her chocolate eyes.

Her hand travels up my thigh and back to my knee.

But I still can't seem to articulate the contours of that ball and how it affects me. Because I have no fucking clue. It was shaped and solidified so long ago.

She continues her soft strokes along my thigh, encouraging me. I have to say something. "Yes, I feel what we have. I…feel that." *I feel your hand. I feel what you do to me. I feel how you help me see, hear, and touch the world.*

"That's good." She strokes again. "So what is it then?"

I'm panting now. Because there's a strange fear clutching my chest, as if I know that somehow I'm going to open up, show my inner workings, because I can feel it crawling up me, even though I don't know its shape.

But it lodges somewhere. I still have no words.

And I need them. But they're stuck and that tightness grows.

Her hand changes its usual course and begins a slow glide up my thigh, and then…oh Jesus, she cups my junk. I grow hard, my dick straining against my jeans. I close my eyes and groan.

"What is it?" she whispers.

She expects me to think? Now? When her hot little hand is stroking my hard-as-fuck cock? I can't think, only feel. But I'm still struggling for words, because I *want* to answer her. She deserves it, even if it's still the wrong thing to say. I have to trust her.

But Jesus God, she's stroking my cock and murmuring and shit, and…oh God, I can't think. I actually—no lie—pull up my torture training. It works for a second. I pull up what I call the blue void—a kind of mental calm blank slate, but then I hear her voice as she murmurs again, and there's no way my brain or body is buying that Pepper is torturing me. She cups the base and strokes up and passes her thumb over the head through the fabric.

"How can you want me if I mess up!" I blurt, the words now unstuck.

Shit.

"Is that what you believe? That you can't ever mess up?"

It's close, but not quite. "I…" I'm mentally groping.

"What does it mean for you to mess up?"

"Disappointment." And more. Pain.

"In yourself?"

"No. Causing it."

She's back to just stroking my thigh, as if she realizes she'd helped dislodge my words and now needs to give me space. "Is that the only emotion you associate with messing up?"

"Rejection. My old man, he'd…he'd punish me if I made mistakes."

Her hand pauses, and then I have a warm handful of Pepper in my lap. She grips my face and forces me to open my eyes and look at her.

Her eyes are alive with emotion, and I can almost see her placing puzzle pieces together, though what the picture is, I still don't know. That terrifies me, but I'm also eager to hear it.

"Are you telling me you feel as if you have to perform to a certain standard in order to be loved?" Her soft voice crosses the space between us and soothes that hurt inside.

Yeah. Shit. I had no idea that's what was inside that messy, messy ball in my chest. It's cracked open and spilling its poison everywhere, and I realize it's all colored by my old man. My old man shaped that ball and lodged it inside me. A ball that said I can't mess up or I won't succeed. Won't be accepted. That ball also said I can't be loved if I mess up.

I'm panting as I stare into her eyes, and I don't dare turn away. And it's not lust. It's fear. That cracked-open ball has left me feeling exposed. My instinct had been right.

She strokes her thumbs over my cheeks and grips my head tighter. "You believe mistakes are a judgment on you. Your worth." Her forehead wrinkles.

I'm feeling my way with this too, but she's sifting through that ball, and she's correctly assessing the situation. I hadn't looked at it that way before, but why would I?

"We all make mistakes," she whispers. "When I point them out, I'm not assigning a judgment to them. It's how you handle a mistake afterward that matters."

She dips down and softly brushes her mouth across mine, and a rush of arousal swamps me, scouring out the poisonous feelings of inadequacy. I groan and clasp my hands around her waist, deepening the kiss.

In the place where that ball had been lodged, I feel a tentative warmth suffusing me, and I relish it. Every dip of my tongue into her mouth is making another tie with her, stitching us together. I slant my mouth to take more of her in. I can't get enough, and I smooth my hands up her waist until I'm cupping the soft curves of her breasts.

A door slams nearby, and we jerk apart.

Shit. It's night time, sure, but Aiden keeps the parking lot lit like a damn football stadium.

She looks at me. "My place."

"Now," I say. "My place is closer, though."

She leaps into her seat, and we both strap in.

LUKE

MY HEART DOESN'T calm down in the short drive from the

bar to my apartment. At my direction, she pulls into the underground garage accessible from the back, and we wind up a level to the resident slots. I'm reduced to grunts by this point, and I motion to the numbered slot between two pillars.

She pulls in, and I hit the button on my seat belt, which whips back with a smack. I reach over to open the door when the *thunk* of the locks engaging fills the small space.

What the—?

I glance over at Pepper, and she gives a cat-in-the-cream smile. I never knew what that really meant. I mean, I got what it was supposed to mean, but I'd never really seen it in a person. Until now.

She puts a finger to her lips. "Shh."

"Pepper…?"

"Luke?" she sing-songs.

She reaches over and brushes her hand just above my waistband, pushing up the hem of my T-shirt. "The way I see it, you feel like you have to perform to get the reward."

Huh? I'm trying hard to listen, I really am. But all the blood has rushed down to the tiny brain that's right below her hand, straining for attention. For *her* attention.

"Here's what's going to happen. We're in a public garage. Anyone could walk by. You're going to sit there and…" She glances around and snags something from the back seat. "And pretend to read this comic."

I'm all kinds of puzzled now, because her hand is stroking me, lust and urgency is streaking through me, and she wants me to read a fucking comic?

"In the dark?"

She glances out the back window and then back at me. She punches the button for the overhead light. "No one's around now. But that can change. You're going to sit there and read this comic and…"

"And?" I croak. I'm completely and totally at her mercy. Clueless, but at her mercy.

"And I'm going to do this." She yanks the snaps of my jeans and…shit…she's…she's not…

Oh shit. She is. Her hair is brushing against my stomach and her warm mouth is caressing the tip of my cock. "Jesus. Fuck." I jerk and glance around. "What the fuck. You can't do this. Not here."

I look down, and she's staring up at me with a wicked gleam in her eye. Totally at odds with the prim bun she's scraped her hair into. "This is for you. Because you're you. Not because you had to earn it or ask for it."

"But…"

But what? She's right, though. I'm mentally flailing because I can't just let her do this to me without me giving back. I'd be nuts to turn down a blow job though. So I reach over and stroke a finger along the small of her back, which is exposed from her stretching over to my seat. Inch under her waistband.

She pulls her lips from my cock. "Nuh-uh. You're reading a comic, remember? Both hands on the comic, held in front of you where anyone can see it."

I stare down at her, completely at her mercy and completely exposed. My breaths are coming in huge gasps, and she purrs. Her tongue darts out and licks the pre-cum from my head. I slam my head back against the headrest. "Fuck." When the hell did my Pepper become a sex kitten?

My whole body is tight as a wire, and I'm vibrating as if I could explode any minute. Taking in several measured breaths I bring the fucking comic up, and my hands…my hands are goddamn *shaking*. I can't tell you what the comic is. It's just a bunch of colored shapes and black lines and chicken scratch.

Her warm hand fondles my balls, and heat streaks up my back. She's stripped me bare, I'm not gonna last long, and her mouth is now clasped around me and slowly taking me all in. So hot. So moist. So tight. Her tongue swirls around on the way back up, and she gives the head an extra suck.

I'm shaking all over. My skin flushes hot, the space around me closes in, and I'm clutching that damn comic like it's the only thing shielding me from an IED. One more deft suck and pull, and that's it. I'm gushing into her mouth as if it's my first time, and I'm quivering and gripping the comic, and I can't do anything but take. Take as she greedily swallows and licks and milks me dry.

Holy fuck.

19

I HURRY ONTO the landing of Luke's stairwell. The same one we hurried through together when I thought he was Rick the Lawyer, and I was channeling my new inner sex vixen.

As before, his heat is at my back, but instead of feeling as if I'm testing a new skin, I'm just *me*. With *him*. And I'm buzzing with excitement and anticipation and other emotions I can't begin to name.

Except…except this is right.

His powerful arm is cinched around my waist, his masculine scent enveloping me. As we turn up the final flight of stairs, I feel a gentle bite on my ear lobe, and his breath tickles my ear with his soft groan. Oh Jesus. I'm already about to crawl out of my skin, I'm so revved up. I don't know how I knew the way to unearth what the heck was going on inside his head, but I'm glad I followed my instincts. Now I'm on fire for him, my panties damp, my clit throbbing.

I'm still trying to process the relief and joy I feel that our talk brought us to this point, and like the first time at the coffee shop, I feel desperate to shore up the gains we made in our discussion by joining in the most intimate way possible.

At the door, Luke fishes his keys from his jeans pocket, and this time I do angle my head and gently bite the bicep bulging right by my cheek.

Cheengk.

The sound of his dropped keys echo in the empty hallway. He growls and picks them up, and I giggle, which earns me a pinch on the butt. Why did I think fully opening myself up would weaken me? I feel as if I can conquer the world.

I glance up as he works his key into the door. His gaze darts to mine, and a huge grin lights up his face. I think my mouth drops open a little, because he looks several years younger.

"Okay, my sex kitten, wait till I get you inside." He winks, pushes open the door, and then I'm in the air, his arms cradling me. He bumps through the opening, flicks on the lights, and slams the door shut with his foot. I'm staring up at his face, and he's looking back with such a hungry but fierce determination that my feet kick in the air, as if it's some kind of reflex action. I swear my lady parts clench.

Without taking his eyes from mine, he strides through his apartment, and I get a tour of the various ceilings behind his head—pebbly, smooth, back to pebbly... Then the ceiling blurs, and I'm airborne.

Bounce.

The sort-of soft cotton of his bedspread teases my calves and arms, and my body dips toward him a bit as he puts his good knee on the mattress. My gaze tracks up to his jean-clad thigh poised inches from me to linger—oh my. Despite the blow job I just gave him, he's sporting an impressive bulge behind his Levi 501s.

"Jesus, Pepper. What you do to me." He grabs himself through the denim and gives a quick tug. Heat flares in my chest and arrows straight down, and I wiggle my legs. Antsy. Desperate.

I bite my lip, hold his gaze, and drag my hand down my stomach. But I don't even get to the place that aches for him, because the next thing I know I'm sliding across his bed, my skirt riding up my back from the friction, his grip tight on my ankle as he pulls me to the edge of the mattress. His gaze darts all over my body, a physical pressure of heat and power and desire sinking into my skin as it passes and turning into a delicious curl of steam, searing down to my core.

"I have to taste you," he says, his voice rumbling with a velvety mixture of iron control and need. Which—God—I don't think I can ever tire of hearing all the nuances his voice might take.

He flips up the front of my pale pink skirt and yanks my panties down to my ankles. I kick them free and open my mouth to say you don't have to reciprocate, but all that emerges is a moan because he shoves my thighs wide and cool air hits my wet folds. He kneels down, and the rough pad of his finger strokes gently across my clit.

Heat flares down my chest, and I'm all nerve endings. I arch upward, needing more friction, needing more. But Luke's having none of it—he clamps onto my waist, holding me tight to his mattress with his strong hands, and drags his tongue lightly through my folds.

I buck. "Please." And then I'm gasping out directions, and he's sucking and pulling and licking, his mouth on me talented and electrifying. I don't worry that he'll think me bossy, or if it'll turn him off, because I know it won't. Joy spreads through me at this freedom, and I gasp. "Harder. Shit. Yeah, right there."

One of his hands leaves my waist, and he presses his thumb across my now-throbbing nub. I writhe. White hot heat coils tighter and tighter, and then I feel his tongue slip into my core. That new freedom is also coiling through me, and I say, "In me. I want you in me when I come."

He flies off me and dives for his nightstand. Before I can blink, he's rolled on a condom. He nudges between my legs, and my whole vision is filled with the beautiful expanse of Luke's broad, muscular chest, his cock jutting upward, thick and hard, and his face set in hard lines. His lids are at half mast, and he falls toward me, landing on his elbows on either side of my shoulders. God—there's nothing like being in the shelter of a brawny male body. And to have it be *Luke's* body?

I whip my legs around his hips, and on a low growl, he thrusts into me so fast and hard that all sensation—all thought—converges to where we're joined, and I'm whispering, "This, this, this," as I feel him, thick and full, inside me.

"Pepper." His eyes are full with wonder and vulnerability.

"Luke," I say, smiling.

He gives a low chuckle, which I can feel vibrate within me where he fills me so completely. I cradle his face and brush my lips across his, and we're languidly exploring with our mouths as he pulls out slowly. I clench around him, protesting the departure, and he rams back into me. I thought I wanted it quick and blinding, because it'd be the only way to fill all the feelings ballooning inside me. However, his movements—a reluctant, slow pull away from me followed by a quick, searing return—are working a different kind of magic, a reward for breaking through to the inside of this man. Now I want to keep having him move inside me in this slow-fast rhythm with his hard length, his odd vulnerability. Forever.

I shudder and cling to him, meeting him stroke for stroke, both of us in sync. But no matter how long I want it to last, I can feel my orgasm inexorably building, so intense and powerful, I want to simultaneously wiggle away from it and wiggle closer. The need to meet it head-on has me shaking all over. Something snaps inside him too, because he grips my face, stares into my eyes, and pistons into me faster and faster, saying my name over and over.

My orgasm bursts through me, but somehow I keep my gaze locked on his. His pupils dilate, his muscles tense, and he thrusts into me one more time. He holds himself still, and I can feel him jerk inside me. Suddenly, I'm hit with a need to protect this man from anything and everything outside of this room. It's a strange feeling, a scary feeling, but I don't shy away from it. He shudders and falls against me, and I grip him as firmly as I can, running my hand up and down his back.

I relish the weight of him as we both fight for breath, my heart beating in my ears. He rolls over and snugs me against him, his strong hand cradling my head against his chest.

I feel as if we've shattered ourselves in multiple ways tonight. Shattered past our fears. Shattered through our barriers that kept the world at a distance. I grip him tighter as I knit my new reality—a reality which includes Luke—into a new shape. I smile.

Q

LUKE

IF WE DIDN'T have to deal with biology, I'd still be in bed with Pepper, but there's no food in my house, and her stomach growled when we woke up this morning tangled in each other's arms. So, yeah, we're back at the Mocha Cabana. Where it all started.

We sit at a different table and dig into our respective, overpriced breakfast sandwiches and fruit. It might be where it all started, but I couldn't feel any more different.

Sure, I still know where everyone is. That's never gonna change. The red mugs are still stupid, though the color is no longer in my face mocking me.

For the first time, I'm completely comfortable in my own skin. I know that, at least with the person sitting across from me, I'm able to be myself. Actually that's not quite right. Before, I wasn't quite…present *inside* me.

I feel an odd lightness, and I can't pin it down until I realize it's the absence of a weight that had always been there. This feeling that I needed to prove myself constantly to be accepted.

I know this isn't a Get Out of Jail Free card or any kind

of bullshit like that. I can't screw up all over the place with her and expect her to just take it like some doormat.

No. But I'm feeling an odd sense of security that if I do my best, even when I mess up, she'll be there.

Trust. It's about trust, which I'd never transferred to a relationship. Before she'd awakened—and her stomach made its presence known—I'd lain in bed holding her, feeling her against me, her sweet scent filling me, and realized that perhaps the pressure for perfection hadn't allowed me room to feel. *She* gives me that room.

Which has me thinking further. "Your idea was a good one."

"Oh, yeah?" She smiles and lifts a cut strawberry, motioning toward my mouth. I part my lips, heart pounding, and she slips it inside. Before her fingers can escape, I give them a quick swipe with my tongue and a wickedly hot spark flares in her eyes.

I clear my throat. "Yeah. Finding a hockey goalie. We were too caught up in wanting to be the best. We let perfection be the enemy of the good. So what if the new guy can't slot in with the same level of familiarity and trust we'd worked so hard to hone."

Her smile lights me up. "At least you'll get to go as a team to the playoffs."

"Exactly." We talk about how we can put out the call for a goalie among the ice hockey, field hockey, and lacrosse circuit. The check comes, and I hand over my card. "You know what my nickname for you was back in high school?"

"Oh God, what?" She chuckles.

"Hot Pepper." And I tell her how I'd fantasized about asking her out.

She wrinkles her nose. "I always hated my name."

"Why?"

"Because I didn't see myself as spicy, or I didn't want to, I guess. Especially once I got to med school—"

"And became Dr. Pepper..."

She groans and rolls her eyes. "Yes, because that's the

first time anyone's teased me with that nickname." She looks down and fiddles with her napkin. "But you know, for the first time I actually…I think I like my name now."

And going with the instinct I always relied on as a SEAL, I reach across and clasp her hand. She glances up, and a bright, warm grin spreads across her face. I catalog this one right along with all the others. I can't wait to bring out more. She squeezes my hand back.

I rub a thumb across her hand. "How do you…how do you know if you love someone?" I can't believe how easily I ask this.

Her eyes go wide, and she sets her napkin down. She puts her hand over mine.

"I'm not sure," she whispers.

"Have you ever…?"

"Nope. You?"

I shake my head and keep my gaze trained on hers. "I'd like to figure it out, though. With you. If you're willing."

There's a suspicious bit of moisture in her eyes, and she nods. "I'm willing. Very willing."

"Well, okay then."

And then I grin, big and wide, and suddenly my heart feels as big as this red café and the city it's in. We're going to do this.

Man, I'm one lucky bastard. Deadpool, my new favorite X-man, would have to agree—Pepper is the right girl to bring out the hero in me.

I pull on her hand until she follows with her body, and I caress her face and seal our promise with a café-safe kiss on those beautiful lips.

THE END

AUTHOR'S NOTE

I HAD A lot of fun writing this story—not only writing a contemporary, but also writing about this little known sport (in our neck of the world). I used to play Gaelic football in the late 90s when I lived in Atlanta, and enjoyed all the friends I made, both Irish and American, and all the *craic* we had! Gaelic football is another Irish sport played with a round ball like a volleyball and looks like a strange mix of soccer, rugby, basketball, and volleyball. It's governed also by the GAA. We were only starting to have a hurling team when I stopped playing, and they hadn't yet formed a camogie team (the name for the women's version of hurling), but I did get to see it played when we went to the different championship games. Since then, it's become much more popular for new clubs to form in America for hurling than it is for Gaelic football.

I grew up in Sarasota, and so I enjoyed highlighting my old hometown. The Purple Chow is fictitious, but is a play on the nickname for the Van Wezel Performing Arts Center, which locals call The Purple Cow. It has the honor of being the world's only purple seashell-shaped theater.

The Mocha Cabana where Luke and Pepper had their coffee date was named by Kate Warren, one of my "assassins"—my fan group Angela's Time-Traveling Steampunk Regency Assassins.

While I was editing this story, Ringling Brothers and Barnum & Bailey Circus announced their decision to close down "The Greatest Show on Earth." John Ringling and the circus were a big part of Sarasota's history. I grew up near the Ringling Museum, a neighborhood that once had—no lie—pink sidewalks. One of my best friends growing up was a granddaughter of Cannonball Zacchinni, one of the brothers who were human cannonballs. In a future book in this series I hope to highlight more of the circus history of Sarasota.

I took liberty with Gainesville having a semi-pro ice hockey team because I needed Phil in the same town with Pepper where she was getting her medical degree. Right now, there are only semi-pro teams in Estero, Orlando, and Pensacola. I could have had him commute from Orlando, but he's too much of a douche to go to that much trouble for someone else.

ACKNOWLEDGEMENTS

I'D FIRST LIKE to thank Olivia Devon for messaging me one day back in October of 2015 asking me if I'd like to be a part of the boxed set SOME LIKE IT GEEK with her and other amazing writers whom I admire. I think I pretty much immediately said yes? This story is a result (originally titled TO SCORE OR NOT TO SCORE).

I'd like to thank the following folks who read early versions and helped me make this a better story! Jami Gold, Shaila Patel, Zoe York, Olivia Devon, Madelynne Ellis, Jinx Kammer, and Anne Marsh. You guys helped me to not only craft a better story, but also helped in the cheerleading department too. Thank you!

I'd also like to thank several of my readers who also read early versions and gave me helpful feedback: Tauline, Megan, and Courtney, thank you!

My editors Gwen Hayes, Jessa Slade, Erynn Newman, and Julie Glover had my back again, which I appreciate so much.

I'd also like to thank Johnny O'Sullivan, who was my former Gaelic football coach. He was so helpful in reading over relevant scenes and making sure I accurately portrayed his native sport. I owe ya one, Johnny!

And to Dr. Harcourt, a local sports med doc, who let me observe him and his staff at the University of South Alabama. He gave me a great run-down of sports medicine and helped me figure out which injuries Pepper, Luke and the rest would sustain. His staff was helpful too.

I also want to thank the members of my facebook fan group—Angela's Time-Traveling Steampunk Regency Assassins—for their help and support! And to Kate who won the contest for naming the coffee shop :)

To Pam, Diane, and the rest of the crew at the Government Street location of Starbucks who keep me supplied in food and tea when I camp out there to write/revise; I get so much work done there and it helps me stay off social media. I wrote and revised most of this book there.

I'd also like to thank my facebook and twitter friends who are always willing to answer questions I pose, whether it's about writing, or character ideas, or an opinion sought.

And finally to my family, who have always believed in me and make it possible for me to pursue writing.

ABOUT THE AUTHOR

Photo by Keyhole Photography

ANGELA QUARLES IS a RWA RITA® Winner and *USA Today* bestselling author of time travel, steampunk, and now contemporary romance. Her steampunk, *Steam Me Up, Rawley*, was named Best Self-Published Romance of 2015 by *Library Journal* and *Must Love Chainmail* won the 2016 RITA® Award in the paranormal category, the first indie to win in that category. Angela loves history, folklore, and family history. She decided to take this love of history and her active imagination and write stories of romance and adventure for others to enjoy. When not writing, she's either working at the local indie bookstore or enjoying the usual stuff like gardening, reading, hanging out, eating, drinking, chasing squirrels out of the walls, and creating the occasional knitted scarf.

She has a B.A. in Anthropology and International Studies with a minor in German from Emory University, and a Masters in Heritage Preservation from Georgia State University. She was an exchange student to Finland in high school and studied abroad in Vienna one summer in college.

Find Angela Quarles Online:
www.angelaquarles.com
@angelaquarles
Facebook.com/authorangelaquarles
Mailing list: www.angelaquarles.com/join-my-mailing-list

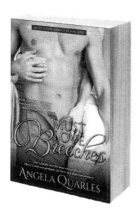

Love Angela's writing style?

Try her time travel series following a modern woman to Regency England!

Purchase *Must Love Breeches* at your favorite retailer in ebook or print format

She's finally met the man of her dreams—too bad he lives in a different century!

A devoted history buff finds the re-enactment of a pre-Victorian ball in London a bit boring...until a mysterious artifact sweeps her back in time to the real event, and into the arms of a compelling British lord.

Isabelle Rochon can't believe it when she finds herself in the reality of 1830's London high society. She's thrilled to witness events and people she's studied. But she may also have to survive without modern tools or career—unless she can find a way to return to her time. And then there's Viscount Lord Montagu, a man whose embrace curls her toes, but who has a dangerous agenda of his own.

Lord Phineas Montagu is on a mission to avenge his sister, and he'll stop at nothing, including convincing an alluring stranger to pose as his respectable fiancé. He's happy to repay her by helping her search for her stolen calling card case that brought her back in time. But he doesn't bargain for the lady being his intellectual match—or for the irresistible attraction that flames between them.

They're both certain they know what they want, but as passion flares, Phineas must keep both himself and Isabella safe from unseen opponents, and she must choose when and where her heart belongs. Can they ever be together for good?

Made in the USA
Columbia, SC
05 October 2017